HIDD[EN]

Even though I [...]
The human ani[mal ...] [o]ff
everything. I didn[...] sex like
the poor limited crea[...] able of tasting
the diversity of the j[...] world.

Yolande was young [and b]eautiful. The day I met
her she had decided to assuage her long-suppressed
desires and offer herself to some woman of little virtue.
Chance threw us together. She looked at me in such
a way that I would have had to be blind not to
understand . . .

Hidden Rapture

and

The Spank 'em Papers

Anonymous

HEADLINE

HIDDEN RAPTURE

CHAPTER I
My Erotic Debut

I am Russian.

Has my life been rich in sexual vicissitudes because of a special erotic temperament, a 'Slavonic nature'? I don't know. Who can say? What I am certain of is that I have had a life filled with passion, excitement, and adventure.

I am an active person, not a meditative one. I was meant to have experiences – numerous experiences – but not to make interpretations or theories. Therefore, I believe I must give the story of my adventures to the world so that those who wish to can make use of them for their abstract development, their synthetic conceptions, and their amoral doctrines.

When I look at the story of my life, I am certain that sensuality played the most essential role. I knew my first happiness thanks to the delights of the body, and my first memories were those of the emotions of onanistic caresses. In boarding school I masturbated in bed and abandoned myself to mad caresses with my little friends who were as shameless as I.

But these larval erotic impulses were to incubate and develop at the skilled and loving hands of the beautiful Madame Ragfan, the directress of our school. She was a strange person, as strange as her name, which seemed less artificial than her appearance, and her inverted nature forced her to disguise herself. Unlike her peers, this woman detested men and adored creatures of her own sex. She had become the directress of an institute for girls so as to be able to better satisfy her lesbian instincts.

As soon as I saw her, I fell in love with her. But at first she paid no attention to me. Was it stimulated or real indifference? Did she have a favorite at the moment who was monopolizing her completely and preventing her from becoming interested in anyone else? I never found out. Madame Ragfan always kept an enigmatic part to her heart – a little box filled with secrets that no one could discover, even in moments of physical abandon.

Despite her detachment in my regard, I continued to look at her in a way that showed the extent of my passion. One day, just after

4

my sixteenth birthday she looked at me as if she had just discovered my penchant for her, and smiled at me. That afternoon, wild with joy, I prayed for our relationship to develop quickly. Then one night, noticing me in the corridor, she came over to me and murmured:

'Come up to my apartment after dinner. I'll wait for you . . .'

My imagination had already foreseen all the details our rendezvous might involve.

I ran outside to the florist whose store was across from the school and bought several roses which were to express the fire in my feelings for Madame Ragfan. Then at the appointed hour, as if in a dream, I walked up the stairs that led to the second floor where she lived. She had put on a silk dress with yellow and blue stripes. I noticed signs of hope and faith in life on her ravishing face. I had never thought I could make a woman as happy as she looked at that moment. Her attitude showed me that she accepted all the risks that our affair would bring.

She undressed me and carried me to the bed as a man carries his wife on their wedding night. She was my husband, my first real husband, and I was her pretty wife. She came to me, kissing me on the chest, on the stomach, on my pussy. Her tongue slid between the lips of my virgin cunt, trying to penetrate as far as possible. Never had any of my schoolmates brought me such pleasure. I was delirious with happiness and desire.

Then Madame Ragfan pulled a leather instrument from under the pillow, that resembled a man's sex — like my father's that I had seen on several occasions — and she tied it to her abdomen with a belt.

'I'm going to deflower you,' she said. 'I don't want to leave your virginity to one of those dirty, barbarian males you will wind up marrying. I want to take you first myself.'

She adjusted her godemiche at the opening of my pussy and started to push it in.

I cried out in pain. She stopped.

'I'm going to make you a woman,' she said. 'Don't you want to become an adult?'

'Yes, my love,' I answered passionately. 'I'm going to be your woman, your wife, your companion for life.'

So she separated my legs in order to reach me better, and attacked again. I bit my lips to keep from moaning. She withdrew and attacked me again. I writhed. The blood was flowing from my cunt down my thighs in an insignificant but continual flow. Madame Ragfan leaned over the long, purple trail and licked it passionately. Then she began her attack again with increasing passion. While she was possessing me, she shouted words that were repugnant and stimulating at the same time.

'So, you like to be fucked, you little whore,' she whispered. 'You like the way I'm enlarging your cunt, don't you? You adore being screwed, I can see that . . . you must have rubbed yourself many times dreaming about blows like this in your crack . . .'

I saw that it pleased her to say such things to me and so I nodded each time, confirming what she wanted to see me admit.

Suddenly I cried out under a more powerful attack. I came. Then Madame Ragfan asked me to suck her cunt, which I did with a certain degree of skill.

Then, on her order, I had to tie the godemiche around myself so I could fuck her, and I had the pleasure of seeing my directress discharge under my assaults. That night we slept together in her bed.

In the morning my love taught me to take care of my face. It was Sunday and we could rest a little longer in her apartment without fear of being disturbed.

I wasn't dressed yet and she was gently caressing my body while I washed myself.

'Your skin is so dull,' she said suddenly. 'Why is that?'

'Oh, I don't know,' I answered. 'Do you think I could still do something about it? Look here, under my eyes; it seems like there are some wrinkles starting to form.'

'Why of course you can do something about

7

it, my dear,' said Madame Ragfan laughing. 'From now on, every day you will use a good cream that I will give you.'

So saying, she got up and went over to a little white closet in which there were many bottles. She took a few out, then decided on a white cream which she began to spread out over my face with a sort of light massage that gave me some very pleasant sensations. She did not forget to moisten my neck, and soon her hands began to descend insidiously toward my plump tits which she caressed, then to my cunt where she began foraging among my hairs. I let her do as she wished because that little lesson in beauty was sufficiently exciting for me to want it to last as long as possible. So that she wouldn't stop, I asked her again:

'Do you think I should oil my eyelids so wrinkles won't form?'

'No, that would be a gross error. An application of oil on the eyelids only accelerates the relaxation and distension of the skin happens soon enough, as it is.'

'But what should I do, then?

'I advise the application of tonics and some serums with a base of embryonic juices. It is only later that a light massage with a thick cream can be effective on wrinkles if there are any.'

I thanked her with a smile. I had turned

toward the mirror to apply the cream and she profited by caressing my back, murmuring:

"We must take care of your back as well. It's so soft, it would be a shame to neglect it.'

Then she slipped her fingers toward my ass and pushed them in gently. She moved slowly, then more quickly, while I continued to work on my face, looking in the mirror and getting terribly excited.

We passed a good part of the morning like that, caressing each other, putting on all sorts of creams and makeup that were terribly exciting.

The next day the Communist Revolution broke out in our little town, which was immediately sacked by laborers, farmers, and intellectual agitators. One of my father's friends came to tell me the awful news, that my parents who lived in St Petersburg, had been arrested and deported to some unknown place. He declared that he was willing to take me to my house or help me get out of the country.

At dawn, with the approval of the directress whom he had visited, I was to leave the school in which I had known my most important amorous revelations. I burst into tears, suddenly realizing that I was going to be separated from my adored mistress. The revolutionary events were going at such a pace that I was afraid I wouldn't even get to see Madame Ragfan before I left. In those tragic hours when fires were breaking out everywhere around us, could she give me a minute of her precious time?

I waited for her in the court. Unable to sleep, I walked up and down, still hoping that she would come to give me a last kiss, a farewell kiss that I would carry with me during my whole life. I was relieved when a hand rested on my shoulder near my neck and pressed my skin gently. What a wonderful surprise to immediately recognize a warm touch! We stood like that for a long time. That hand weighing on my neck gave me a desire to live because it overpowered me with pride.

One last time we came face to face in the dark without being able to see each other, she looking fixedly at my head, searching for my face. She wasn't leaning against me; there was no desire for possession in our movements. It was a sad moment and I tried to express my feelings. True lovers leave each other many times before each parting, and I understood very well that Madame Ragfan desired a farewell accompanied by a romantic night of magic. It seemed as though I could hear her breath, feel the beating of her heart. Her fingers suddenly began to move on my neck, playing an invisible scale. I trembled.

I had recognized her without fear, and now I found desire rising in me again. I suddenly felt a bursting of feeling that I had thought dead, a birth of kisses that were old, of caresses that had seemed buried. Her hand was moving again, sliding toward my ear. She knew all the weaknesses in my armature, all my erotic zones, all the secret veins where desire burned. She was naked under her dress, standing there in the fog – I gritted my teeth.

Memories were beginning to dance in my body. My mouth recalled the sacred dryness of the first kiss we had exchanged several hours earlier. Everything was beginning again.

My body, aroused and expectant, was vibrating with impatience. I was about to move blindingly into the midst of the future. I would go to her, feel her breath on my neck, her desire on my back. We would start to walk, she would suddenly be at my side, and we would go to bed without hurrying, free, gifted with nuptial patience. It was then that I understood how she could overcome destiny, make me do anything, keep me prisoner. I went over to her and murmured:

'My darling.'

She trembled. I bit my lip and smiled.

'My love!'

'Yes,' she said, beaming.

I made her turn around, put my arm around her and pressed her to me, placing my lips on hers. I felt a forceless fury in her. I would have liked to take her wildly, crush her body stiff with emotion against mine, but suddenly her supple abdomen melted against me and her tongue ran softly over my gums. Welded to me, soft, I succeeded easily in bending her. Then beauty became vulgarity, adorable vulgarity impregnated with spiritual love. She took her godemiche, tied it to her abdomen, and fucked me with it until I came in tears.

Then she gave me the tool that was still moist with my vaginal juices and asked me to fuck her in the ass. I took her with all my juvenile strength, and she also discharged. We parted at dawn. I never saw my initiator – my unforgettable initiator – again.

CHAPTER II
The Brothers

When I went back to St Petersburg with my father's friend, I found no traces of what had constituted my former life. My father and mother had disappeared, our house was occupied by strangers – responsible officials of the new regime – our servants had left for their villages, and everyone treated me like a stranger, even chased me away.

Soon I also lost the man who had brought me to the town. He was arrested or killed in one of the unexpected and brief battles between the Whites and the Reds who were still fighting.

I found myself alone in the world. I wandered through the streets, terrified and famished. A man took me home with him and violated me. At least he gave me a bed and some food as recompense, and I became his mistress. One of his friends who was much younger and more attractive talked me into

13

abandoning my lover and accompanying him out of the country to a place where he had – at least he said he had – friends and family.

My life had been repugnant to me. This new friend represented a ray of hope, so I followed him, and a train packed with refugees became our only home for many long days.

Two weeks later when I got off, I was again alone, having lost my new companion on route during one of the many station arrests. My sole possession was a bottle of vodka I had gotten from a soldier in exchange for a quarter hour of pleasure.

'I'd like to screw you, baby,' he had said.

'Not in this life,' I replied. 'Do you want me to catch the clap? What would I do then?'

He took the bottle of alcohol out of his torn pocket and showed it to me.

'This, in exchange for one fuck. OK?'

I didn't hesitate, already cynical and hardened by the times.

'That's worth the clap!'

When our train stopped, he screwed me against the wall of the abandoned station. I was lucky he didn't have any diseases. After I left the train, I traveled onto the other end of the Ukraine.

Night had already fallen when I timidly knocked at the first door I saw. A young man,

Yvān, opened it and the wind rushed in, a dry, glacial wind that sprinkled the floors with powdered snow. The grandfather swore, the grandmother coughed, and the little lamp she was holding on her lap began to bleat. Then Pavel, Yvan's brother, laughed that stupid, cruel, Russian laugh that always unnerved me.

'Come in,' he said.

I entered, thanked him, and took off my bonnet and cloak.

Everyone looked at me curiously. Visitors were rare in that forgotten village on the Polish border. I explained that I was going to another village several miles away but that the snow had caused me to stop and that I wanted to spend the night with them. No one asked me who I was, contented only that I wasn't a policeman. The police and investigators who wanted to find out about their resources in livestock and crops apparently never came alone.

The grandmother wasn't happy, however. She was about to serve the evening meal and now they would have to invite a stranger. I sat down before the stove, being careful not to disturb anyone, and dried my boots and clothes. The odor of the smoky lamps, of leather and wet clothes, and of nearby stable, formed a foul stench. Yvan left to milk the cow and asked his brother to come help him.

15

When he refused, I decided that this would
be an opportune moment to offer my help.
Therefore I accompanied him to the stable.
He gave me the lantern and made a sign for
me to hold it so that he could see what he was
doing. While he milked, he never took his
eyes off me. Suddenly he asked me to trade
jobs with him. I agreed. As soon as his hands
were free, he began to caress my braids and,
in a voice that was sweet, yet very virile, he
asked me how old I was and whether I had
been annoyed by any soldiers on the road.

'No,' I replied.

He seemed relieved and, looking at me and
smiling, he took a leather purse out of his
pocket. Inside the purse was a little box
which he handed to me.

'Here, take it, it's yours. You were so nice
to help me.'

Inside the box was a tiny gold ring with a
little red stone. I could only put it on my little
finger. The jewel looked like a drop of blood.
I had never seen such a beautiful ruby. I
blushed when I put it on my finger and went
back to milking the cow. I could feel Yvan's
warm breath on my neck. I lowered my head,
and he placed a furtive kiss on my naked
neck.

Suddenly Pavel came in. He laughed, made
a crude joke, and pulled on my tits,
pretending to milk them. Then he pulled me

into his arms. I struggled, but as my hands were occupied, he soon got my blouse open to reveal my deliciously plump breasts.

My cheeks turned purple. I let go of the cow, threw my fist at him, and caught him in the face. I tried to hit him again, but Yvan held me back. I tried to rebutton my blouse but my hands were still trembling with outrage. If I hadn't been so afraid of the strong wind, I would have immediately run away into the night.

When Pavel left, Yvan buttoned my blouse, but not without first testing the beautiful fruit that I permitted him to admire in the palm of his hand. He rubbed my nipples with his fingertips and began to gently lead me to the house. The big common-room was empty and Yvan drew me to the rustic staircase that led upstairs. We were holding hands; his fingers held mine tightly, and I pressed his even more tightly. His eyes had changed and he was looking at me with a glazed expression. We went up to a tiny room, a kind of lumber room or loft with a floor covered with straw. We stretched out silently and our two bodies disappeared in the denseness of the straw. I was flattered by the attention that the man was giving me, by the feeling I was creating in him. I was a little ashamed of myself, but my desire was too strong. Suddenly I felt Yvan's hand grab mine and lead it gently toward his crotch. The darkness was so complete in our refuge that I could not see his member growing harder and harder in his pants. He forced me to caress him there a little, then asked me to unbutton him. I did so immediately and his rod jumped out, hard as a steel sword. The strength and the dimensions of his prick surprised, even stupefied me. Yvan increased the pressure of his fingers on mine so that I would caress his hard cock. Then suddenly, he stretched out on top of me and covered my face and body with passionate kisses. I continued to rub his cock, excited by imagining how the stiffness of his tool would feel inside me.

I heard my lover murmur endless phrases whose meaning I could not grasp. I felt his saliva inundating my neck, but instead of feeling disgust, it excited me even more. His hand was moving up my leg, under the elastic of my panties. He was already beginning to grope in my cunt. I was writhing passionately and rubbing his stick even more frantically. His fingers were touching the most sensitive parts of my cunt. I was mad with pleasure, although I kept telling myself that I shouldn't abandon myself to the first emotion that a stranger made me feel. But this desire was stronger and I impulsively jerked on my partner's cock faster and faster. Meanwhile, Yvan's fingers were penetrating further and further into my dilated slit and soon we were sharing an equal pleasure of the senses.

My hand descended from his cock to his balls and I felt them as if to evaluate their weight. Then I moved up again toward his abdomen, overwhelmed by sensations I had never felt before.

'Oh, it's good! Your cunt is wonderful, you know,' murmured Yvan.

I pushed myself against him and moved so that his fingers could reach me better. My partner's member was trembling in my hand. Suddenly he stopped moving his hands and I felt his rod standing up in my hand, ready to burst. He let out a brief moan and a flood of sticky come flowed over my wrist. With this erotic sensation, and under the increasing pressure of his fingers, I answered with a discharge that made me tremble all over and answer his moan with a cry of joy.

Several minutes later we went downstairs. The dinner went better than I had expected. I still had the bottle of vodka in my pocket and I offered it to them. The grandmother and grandfather had not had a drink in several months and they enjoyed it tremendously. Pavel pinched my thighs under the table, but I didn't dare stop him.

As for Yvan, he never took his eyes off me. After the meal we went up to bed. The two brothers shared the same room, each in a corner on a pile of hay, while I occupied the next room. I stretched out, still dressed because I didn't have a nightgown.

I couldn't fall asleep. All I could think about was Pavel. I saw myself in the stable again. I kept thinking of that boy pulling on my breasts as I had been pulling on the cow's udders. What surprised me was that it had been the youngest of the brothers who had dared to do it. My hands wandered over my breasts and suddenly my fantasy changed. Now it was Yvan caressing me. His fingers were as gentle as his eyes. I imagined him undressing me, contemplating my naked body. The wind was howling outside. It was shaking all the branches with a monstrous force. The lamp had been extinguished and the room was as dark as an oven. The alcohol was warming me more than it had before. In the dark everything smelled like wet dogs. To escape from the odor, I opened my blouse and breathed the perfume of my own skin. A strange and powerful desire that I had rarely felt was growing in my body.

I sighed deeply. Someone was pushing the door gently open and coming toward me. Had that sigh awakened one of the sleepers?

'Be quiet,' said a barely perceptible voice. 'Don't wake the others.'

I couldn't see his face or his body, but I felt him moving over to me and stretching out beside me. Then I felt his fingers touch my forehead and caress my cheek. I thought it must be Yvan and yet he seemed less gentle than before dinner in the stable. Was it young Pavel? I wanted it to be the older one. I pressed his hand. The strange palm stiffened. It descended into my half-opened blouse, seized my breasts, and began caressing them just like in my dream. The hand had become demanding and hard. Yet, despite the strangeness, this rough handling was delightful. *Was* it Pavel?

Now the hand descended from my breasts to my legs. I knew that my desires were going to be satisfied; still, I feared what was to follow.

When I suddenly felt a body moving heavily on mine, the pressure of a stiff cock against me was a voluptuous torture which I could no longer resist.

Suddenly a ray of moonlight permitted me to recognize my lover – it was Pavel. But how ruthless and handsome he was in his nocturnal desire, like an adorable naughty child. He squeezed me and looked into my eyes. It seemed as though we had renounced words entirely, to sense our actions more completely. My lover ran his hands all over me, from my chest to my stomach. He watched me with a wild expression on his face and, although he was hurting me, he was exciting me terribly. I wanted him to crush me, and I put my own arms around him and drew him to me. Then our lips were united and welded together with a perfection that intoxicated us.

I felt my cunt filling with a warm liquid as Pavel continued to cover me with kisses. He bit my lips and pushed his tongue against mine. I began to unbutton his shirt with nervous fingers. I wanted to press his young chest against my breasts. It was the first time I had undressed a man. I pressed my mouth to his soft skin. He sighed and half-closed his eyes with obvious passion.

When I had almost completely undressed him, Pavel clumsily but firmly took off my panties. We both were completely naked. He had a magnificent body and his cock was pointing maliciously outward from the juncture of his splendid thighs. I loved his prick. I took it in my hand and began to caress it. Instinctively I leaned over and kissed it gently. It was a real pleasure to put it in my mouth, to suck it, and even to bite it. Pavel closed his eyes and sighed ecstatically. Then I stopped eating him because I wanted him inside me.

'Come, my darling . . . take me . . .' I murmured, opening my legs for him. I was wild with desire, waiting for Pavel's cock to come into my opened flesh. But Pavel murmured kissing my abdomen, 'No, I prefer to take you from behind.'

After saying these words, he covered me with kisses. I was a little surprised and asked,

'Why? Don't you like to fuck?'

'No, I prefer it the other way. In the village we are often only among boys and it isn't possible to do it any other way.'

I was stupefied by this revelation, but instead of repulsing me, the discovery that Pavel liked to fuck in the rear excited me even more.

'Well, then wouldn't you like to make love the normal way, the way you should with a woman?'

'It's just that I'm so accustomed to the other way that I wouldn't be very good at anything else.' I smiled, amused, as he continued.

'I only have one desire: to take you from behind.'

His eyes were deep, and filled with lust. He turned me around brutally. Then he leaned over my ass and touched it gently as he put a finger into me. He kissed my shoulders, then his mouth descended along my back and I felt his tongue inside me. I was swooning with pleasure under these soft caresses. He continued to lick the inside of my ass and I began to move a little so that his tongue could penetrate me more deeply.

'Come, I beg you . . . I'm yours, do it now! You've made me want it!'

He leaned over me and placed his rod between my buttocks. When he entered me I moaned with pain because his cock was as long as it was hard and I was really suffering. But at the same time, I was already beginning to feel the pleasure that he was giving me.

'Oh, it's good!' I whispered. 'I love this! Oh, it's good!'

My words excited him and he pushed his cock further into me. He began to fuck me wildly, like an animal, and I couldn't feel the pain anymore. An immense joy was invading every fiber of my body. I was trembling with passion.

My lover was growing heavier and heavier and his blows reverberated deep in my loins; the savagery with which he was attacking me was giving me fantastic pleasure.

'Bitch, you like taking it in your ass!' he whispered. 'You like having your ass penetrated by a big cock like mine! You love it, don't you . . .'

His words, spoken in a vulgar voice, stimulated me even more. I answered,

'Yes, bastard, I like it! I like the way your cock fills me up! I love this! You're going to break my insides, but I'm happy. You're giving me so much pleasure!'

He moaned deeply.

'I love your ass! It was made to be fucked.'

'I kept it for you, my darling. I knew that I would meet you and that one day you would take me from behind.'

He was moving faster and faster and I was melting with joy. He dug his nails into my ass and I felt the pain only as pleasure. His balls were slapping against my ass and the dull sound it made excited me enormously. I could feel my orgasm coming and all I needed to discharge was a slightly stronger thrust of his cock. As if Pavel had guessed my thoughts, he started to charge me with unimaginable rage. I wasn't even able to cry out when I finally came. I could only let out a long moan and Pavel, feeling me discharge, answered with his own, deep-throated cries. I felt his member growing harder and harder in my burning ass, tearing the walls inside me. Finally he groaned, 'I'm coming! I'm coming! Oh, yes, it's good. I'm coming.'

He pressed my buttocks again while he spilled his sperm into my ass.

We were silent for some time and then he started to get hard again. I thought we ought to couple normally now. Pavel was a tremendously exciting lover and I only had one desire left – for him to take me in his arms again and cover my face and body with passionate kisses. I felt his stiff cock resting against my ass and that sweet contact excited me even more. It was obvious that he still didn't have the courage to fuck me so I decided to take the initiative.

'Come on,' I murmured, 'take me, fuck me now the way you should fuck a woman!'

He crushed himself against me. I felt his prick against my vagina, but he was so nervous that he couldn't adjust it properly. I seized it and gently introduced it into my hole.

'Push it in, my love! You're going to fuck me! I'm trembling already! Push it in, I beg you!' He pushed it in, hard, and soon was fucking me brutally. His wildness made me delirious. He leaned on my shoulders and attacked me more and more forcibly. He was panting and the sweat was running over his temples.

'Oh, it's good to fuck this way.' He cried out. 'I love it! I'm hurting you, aren't I? You love it! Oh, it's good! I love your cunt! Oh, it's wonderful!'

I was filled with ecstasy and pride when I heard these words, for I knew that I was his first woman.

'Tell me, darling, do you like doing this?' I asked.

'Yes, it's good. I like fucking this way because I can see your eyes, know your desires, and guess everything that is in your heart!'

Our senses were so wildly excited that we

were like two animals trying together to know the most delicious of ecstasies. Our tongues lashed at each other while he fucked me; we were like a single body in the same vertigo of the senses. We were panting in unison and our sweat was mingling. I was in pain, because Pavel was so wild. My cunt had been so used by his fingers and cock that it felt as though it was on fire, but all the pain only excited me more. I was writhing on the hay and moaned as Pavel inundated me with his sperm.

I left the house the next morning accompanied only by Yvan. His brother, Pavel, was exhausted and still in bed.

The elder boy had promised to take me to the border and now he was keeping his word:

'You slept with Pavel,' he said with a sad smile.

'Yes,' I answered.

'What's the difference,' he remarked without losing his smile. 'We are all sinners, that is to say, angels who have lost their way.'

He led me to a hill and showed me the road that stretched out on the other side.

'Beyond the hill is Poland.'

I kissed him tenderly.

'Good luck, Svetlana!'

'Good luck, Yvan!'

When I turned around I could see Yvan's silhouette against the distant, gray sky.

A half hour later I had left Russia.

CHAPTER III
The Voyeur

One month later I was in Paris.

Forced to earn my living and knowing no other trade, I became a prostitute. The strangest adventure, or rather the most enlightening, took place one week after my arrival.

When I first met the old man, he seemed preoccupied, a little worried, and yet very easy to converse with . . .

It was in a little street in the Bois de Bologne, surrounded with the calm of sunset. He was walking in the same direction as I, and just when I was about to pass him I realized that he was going to walk alongside me. Suddenly he stopped short.

'Where are you going?' I asked. He hesitated an instant, then answered:

'At the moment, I'm staying here. I'm waiting for someone. If you aren't in a hurry, stay here, don't run off . . .'

'Oh,' I joked, 'you're impatient for some young woman who is making you wait!'

'No . . . yes . . . I mean, yes and no . . .'

I started to laugh.

'You're not quite sure, are you?'

'Yes, yes,' he affirmed. 'I really am waiting for someone, but that person isn't late . . . she's there.'

And he showed me two lighted windows on the first floor of the house we were standing in front of.

'I understand,' I said. 'You're watching her and you can't leave for fear of missing something.'

'No, no, I can't miss her, because as soon as she comes out she'll look for me.'

I didn't understand anything in his enigmatic story, but it appeared to me that my companion had as much, if not more, of a desire to explain what he was doing there than I had curiosity to hear it. I didn't have to question him further because he continued.

'It's very complicated – and quite natural for you not to understand what I'm doing in this street. I have a little friend, a lovely young girl who is hardly twenty . . . that might surprise you because of my gray hair. I won't hide the fact that I have passed fifty. But one only ages in his arteries and I pride myself on being closer to thirty in the area of amorous passion. That is, you will agree, the best age for love because one tastes better, one appreciates more deeply, more exquisitely, the perfume of the adorable flowers that one gathers . . .'

My companion seemed to grow young as he talked. From his grave voice suddenly came a sound of sensual ardor as he sang a hymn to love.

'Of course youth goes away at a mad speed. The seduction of a man like me is more secretive, more refined, perhaps. To succeed in conquering a beautiful young girl's heart and senses, we who no longer have a young boy's smooth fresh skin, fresh lips, or young blood in our veins must use much more skill and much more wisdom. Fortunately, we are rich in experience and know how to put it to good use. All this is to tell you that I still have a chance of finding beautiful girls who know how to appreciate what I can still offer them. Happily so!' he cried with a kind of exalted fervor. 'Without that, existence would be tasteless to me. I think I would no longer have the strength to live a single day in which the joys of love were denied me!'

Suddenly he stopped, looking up at the lighted windows.

'I thought I heard a call, but I guess I was wrong. Anyway, it's better that I stay here. You never know what's going to happen.'

31

So saying, he posted himself under the window.

'I'm happy I'm not alone at the moment. It's less risky when there are two. You don't hear anything, do you?'

'No, why do you ask?' I replied.

Lifting his head and not taking his eyes off the lighted windows, he added, 'You see, I promised to intervene at the smallest call and it was only with this promise that she consented to come here.'

I looked at the old man. He seemed a little bewildered, but passionately attentive. He kept his eyes fixed on the window almost ecstatically.

Unconsciously I began to share his vigil and stood watch as well without knowing what I was waiting to see. I knew that what was keeping me there with the strange man whose actions and movements seemed inexplicable to me was only profound curiosity.

My companion suddenly became obstinately quiet and I felt that all the questions I might ask would have been useless. If I wanted an explanation, I would have to stay with him at all costs. I can't say exactly how long we remained, standing next to one another, impatient, nervous, not caring about the searching, questioning looks we got from passersby.

Suddenly my friend jumped. A graceful young woman with a supple body and light step had just come out. He took her by the arm, pulled her to him.

'Come with us,' he said to me.

I followed them. They were walking very quickly, tenderly pressed against each other. The young woman said a few words every once in a while, and I piped up:

'You'll tell me everything that's happening soon, won't you . . . you won't forget! You swear it?'

We went into a cafe and sat down in a little room at the back where we could be alone. The lovers seemed intoxicated with each other, Without paying any attention to me, the old man leaned toward his lover and said:

'Now, tell me, tell me . . . What did he say when you got there?'

'He told me that my hair was like gold thread used in the Church, that I was like a goddess; that I was going to preside over the service that was to be celebrated by my cult, that I should let things happen and had nothing to fear, but that I shouldn't let anything surprise me. When he spoke to me his words almost resembled litanies. Then I suddenly felt light hands taking my clothes off. Two women dressed in long blue tunics were undressing me with such skillful and precise movements that I was hardly aware of it. There was soft music in the background and the smell of incense created an atmosphere which was beginning to excite me strangely. Then I heard some words being mumbled by a serious voice. All I could make out was the word, Astarte. When I was completely naked, they had me stretch out in a kind of long box lined with blue silk that was in the shape of a coffin . . .'

'Completely naked?' her aging lover asked eagerly.

'Yes, yes, of course . . .'

'And what was Pierre, the bishop, doing?'

'He joined his hands in a kind of prayer, then he knelt down before me with his face to the ground. I saw the two women lean over me and dangle a kind of small incense box from which something that looked like a teaspoon was hanging and which was tied to a censer by a chain. After they had balanced all their tools over my head and while Bishop Pierre engaged in some genuflexions, they disappeared for a second and returned with two big baskets covered with blue silk.'

'Two big baskets? What was in them?'

'Blue and yellow rose petals which they proceeded to spread out all over me. They smelled delicious and felt so soft as they fell on my naked body.'

The old man was listening to all these details, almost ghoulishly savoring them while he slowly caressed his companion's neck and arms. She continued:

'When my body was covered with rose petals, the bishop, who was on his knees, suddenly got up, came toward me, then knelt again and kissed my feet with such passion that I was beginning to be frightened. If I had been alone with him, and if there hadn't been two women next to us, burning perfumes whose odorous smoke was enveloping us like a cloud, I think that I would have called you as you had told me to do.'

'You can be sure that I would have come at the first call as I promised you. At one moment I thought I heard your voice.'

'Yes, that's possible because I let out a cry when I suddenly saw the bishop writhing on the ground as if he were suffering an attack of epilepsy. But one of the young women leaned toward me and murmured gently in my ear, "Don't be afraid! This won't last long."

'Soon the man got hold of himself and broke into tears near my coffin. Then, again contemplating me with religious fervor, he took the petals that were covering me in his hands and smelled them deliriously. He rubbed them over my body again, letting them fall back on me like rain, then gathered them up again. This little game lasted a long time. I felt like laughing because this comedy seemed so ridiculous to me and I was beginning to hate being stretched out in the bottom of that box, without moving, while these affectations went on. I wondered how long it would last, knowing that you were getting impatient. But there was that wonderful smoke, that soft music, and the women who were doing these strange things as if they were the most natural actions in the world. I think they must be quite used to those ceremonies. Finally the lights went out completely. At that moment a door opened and several people came in, advancing in precise rows. The men were dressed in black robes like monks. The women were wearing white nuns' robes. They all formed a little circle around us, crossed their hands over their chests, and murmured a prayer, the words of which were indistinct. Their faces filled with religious fervor.

'Finally Bishop Pierre took the cross and, parting my vaginal lips with it, stuck it in me like a cock. Then, while he poked me with the cross, he began to sing an Ave Maria. As he continued to recite prayers and to scrape my cunt, the bishop also kissed my nipples and stomach from time to time, and in spite of myself, I began to utter little moans of pleasure.

'The man of God continued his mass. Suddenly he withdrew the cross and replaced it with his tongue. This filled me with new excitement and he began to lick my clitoris. Then I felt the bishop's hand grab mine and lead it slowly to the place of his excitement. I seized his swollen cock and began to rub it. It was with an extraordinary pleasure that I caressed the bishop's stiff prick as he continued to suck me. I was writhing and moaning while his tongue darted inside me. I was panting and dizzy from the unsatisfying sensations he was giving me. Now I desired a more complete penetration.

'The bishop must have understood my desires because he soon withdrew his tongue and moved over me. I soon had his old face against mine and it disgusted me a little. But the desire to come overwhelmed me. His cock was very big and penetrated me divinely. Finally I knew the supreme spasm and lay back satisfied. In the delirium of the flesh I forgot where I was. It seemed that I was lying in a bed just being fucked. The bishop must have felt the same ecstasy because his face was twisted in pleasure and the saliva was dripping over his chin. Then he came. I was getting excited again and I tried to encourage him to speak.

' "You like this, bastard? You wanted to

fuck me, didn't you? You like putting your big prick into me!''

' "Yes, whore, I like it. You were meant to be fucked with a dick like mine!''

'Yes, but could you do it again at your age?'

' "Yes, it's because of my erotic strength that I was elected bishop of the rite of Astarte. All you have to do is suck me a little and you'll see how big I'll get again!''

'I obeyed and seized his gland between my lips. Several minutes later he was ready to fuck again.

' "I can possess you again, divine creature!'' he said in a proud voice.

' "Then do it, dirty priest, fuck me harder!''

' "You're marvelous,'' he murmured. "Now, according to the rites, I must spit in your face while I'm possessing you.''

'That repulsed me a little, but the bishop was exciting me so much that I acquiesced.

' "Do what you want! I'm yours. Spit on me, on my tits, on my abdomen, on my cunt, everywhere! Spit on me, I deserve it!''

'Then the bishop looked at me and while penetrating me with his enormous phallus, began spitting on my face. I felt his balls pressing against me and I shouted with pleasure at the same time as the priest continued to spit on me. I was delighted with the methods he was using. We were both on the verge of discharging.

' "I'm going to come," I almost shouted. "Fuck me harder, I want to come."

' "Yes, yes. I, too. I feel my cock swelling up inside your cunt! It's divinely good!"

'The violence of his blows increased and I trembled at the idea of the extreme pleasure I was going to know, thanks to him. Finally I began writhing under the last thrusts, and I moaned with joy and pain. At the same time, the bishop leaned over me and came inside me. We were silent for a few moments, savoring our pleasure. I was waiting with curiosity and a little fear for the next event. The bishop got up and one of the priests who had been watching our coupling came over to him with gold cup filled with water and began to clean my lover's cock. Then it was my turn to be washed. The priest separated my thighs and began to stroke my cunt with a white lace handkerchief. When he had finished, the bishop turned to his followers and said:

' "Now that I have fucked your sister, you can do with her as you wish. She belongs to all of you."

'I was a little stupefied. I remained stretched out on the altar as the bishop had ordered me to do and the line of followers began. All the men and women of the assembly passed before me. Some of them touched me, others moved by indifferently.

Some slid their hand over my slit as if to measure it. Palms caressed my breasts, my hair, and my buttocks. They all made erotic propositions to me. At first I refused but as there was a great number of people and as each had excited me a little, it wasn't long before I was answering their caresses. First, those of a magnificent athlete. However, we had to wait for fulfillment until the procession had ended. I accepted a second offer from a young girl of about seventeen who begged me to play with her pussy. She had such pretty black eyes that I could not resist. Then I let myself be tempted by another man.

'When the procession finally ended, I was free. In a corner of the room I found the three people to whom I had promised myself. As I greeted them, the handsome athlete pulled me to him, pressed me against his strong chest and covered me with passionate kisses, biting my nipples in passing. Under his clothes he was naked and it was very easy to slide my hand in and grab his enormously dilated cock. I couldn't rub him because he was too excited and didn't allow me the time. He had already lifted my legs and was screwing me with his enormous phallus. While the handsome man was fucking me, the young girl was rubbing her pussy against my ass. The third of my admirers contented himself with watching us for the moment.

'I felt the athlete's cock growing in my cunt and soon he inundated me with his sperm. As soon as he was finished, he got up and went over to join a group of men and women who were fucking and licking each other. I was very disappointed because I was really very excited and would have loved my partner to stay with me.

'The young girl continued to caress my ass but she didn't stay with me for long because a young priest took her into a corner of the room and started fucking her. She accepted this rape with obvious pleasure. Thus I was all alone with the last of my partners who was looking at me with an arrogant smile. I looked straight back at him and started to get up to go over to a couple who seemed to be enjoying themselves immensely. He stopped me and, still smiling, murmured:

' "Stay with me. I'm a good man and I'll make you taste the most intoxicating joys of the flesh." He seized me by the shoulders and pressed me to him.

' "Come, don't stay here with all these people. I don't like to make love in a crowd!"

'Almost hypnotized, I followed him without any resistance. He led me into a long corridor at the end of which was a little room rustically furnished with a white wood bed, an identical commode, and several armchairs covered with colored cushions. As soon as we entered the room he grabbed me and kissed me on the mouth. It was one of those long kisses that makes you tremble all over, certain that your lover is very attracted to you. Then, pushing me away almost brutally, he whispered:

' "Now that we're alone, I'm going to really enjoy you!"

'I trembled a little, fearing his words, but I would have consented to anything he wanted to do. He ran his hands over my body as if he wanted to know all its curves. He dug his nails into my breasts, then my abdomen, and finally stopped at the entrance to my cunt. I thought he was going to caress me a little and I instinctively separated my thighs. But his fingers did not penetrate my cunt. He contented himself with just touching me lightly. Finally my partner let go of me.

' "There now, you're ready, you're sufficiently excited to accept anything. Now I'm going to whip you, you dirty little whore!"

' "Do with me as you wish! I'm yours," I whispered.

'Then he went over to the commode and took out a long leather whip. He came very close to me and began to touch my nipples with it. This sensation excited me and it was I who cried:

' "Now, beat me, I beg you, you bastard. Punish me. Beat my stomach, my cunt, everything! Please!"

'He began beating me very gently as if he were caressing me. His blows gradually became harder. I was panting and rolling on the bed on which he had pushed me. Now the whip was moving over my whole body and red marks were beginning to appear on my skin. My joy was immense. My partner was gritting his teeth and a sticky phlegm was flowing from his mouth over his chin and then onto my body. I saw his cock stiffen as he whipped me. I continued to shout:

' "Fuck me, beat me harder, I can't stand it anymore. Hurt me more, I beg you! Oh, it's so good, you're marvelous!"

'Suddenly, incapable of holding back. I stiffened and discharged.

' "I'm coming! I'm coming! I'm coming!"

'I let myself fall back on the bed as my partner, who had not yet known the final pleasure, ordered:

' "Now that you have discharged, you must whip me! But I like to have two people on me. I have to have someone sucking my cock. I'm going to look for Brother Daniel who usually serves as my partner."

'With that, he disappeared from the room and then returned, accompanied by a big man of about thirty with a dark complexion.

43

My partner immediately held out the whip to me.

' "Now, avenge yourself. Beat me, whip me, you little whore. As for you, Brother Daniel, suck my cock! But hurry, both of you!"

'His companion knelt down, seized the flagellant, and began to suck his prick. As for me, I began to beat my ex-punisher with all the strength I had left. We didn't continue that way for long because my lover suddenly decided that I should sodomize Brother Daniel while he continued to suck him. In order to accomplish my new task he asked me to put on a godemiche that was in the commode. I obeyed, and armed with my tool, I began buggering Brother Daniel who shouted as soon as I penetrated him. While I screwed the brother's ass, I began to beat the first man again. Suddenly Brother Daniel discharged. Seeing him tremble and cry out with joy, I discharged in my turn. Only the flagellant, who was watching us, his nostrils trembling, his forehead covered with sweat, had not discharged yet. I went over to him and grabbed his cock that was ready to burst. I put it in my mouth and caressed his ass with my free hands. I didn't have to suck him for long because soon I felt a sticky liquid flowing into my mouth, which I hastened to swallow in gratitude to the man who had whipped me.'

* * *

The old man and I were listening with mixed emotions as the young girl told of these orgies. I was stupefied and excited; the man was breathing heavily, his body stiff with lust.

'And then what happened?' he asked.

'That's all!' answered his delightful friend. 'Except that when I was about to leave the apartment, a woman slipped a check for five thousand francs into my hand, saying, "My lord Bishop was very satisfied and told me to ask you if you would come again Thursday." '

'And?'

'Well, I accepted! Five thousand francs is always a good thing to have. Next time I'll be prepared and you won't have to stand guard under the window.'

'No, no, I'll be there,' cried her lover. 'You never know what's going to happen! I won't be able to relax knowing you're all alone. And now that I know all about it, I could follow the ceremony in my thoughts. The rite will probably always be the same.'

The old man licked his greedy lips. Then, looking at me, he said:

'We even forgot to introduce ourselves. Permit me to repair my omission. This splendid woman next to me is Marie-Anne and my name is Legros, George Legros.'

'My name is Svetlana Roubetzky,' I answered. 'I am of Russian origin.'

'Oh, perfect,' said our companion. 'I haven't had a Russian girl for a long time.'

Then he called the waiter, paid the bill, and got up.

'Where are we going?' I asked.

'Why, to my studio . . . We'll make love there because I'm really in the mood.'

'I am, too,' I replied. 'I hope you'll be generous to a woman like me who earns her living by sleeping with men. But can Marie-Anne get excited again after her recent experiences?'

'Oh don't worry about me,' answered Marie-Anne brightly. 'I'm a real nympho-maniac. I can go on all day and all night. I know how to come over thirty times in a single day!'

I had heard about such creatures, capable of coming practically without resting, but I was actually meeting one for the first time. I would be happy to spend a few hours in her company. Mr Legros hailed a taxi that took us to his home. During the ride we kissed and caressed each other.

Our host's studio was simply and charmingly furnished. It was a proper setting for the refined man to whom the practice of love remains an art.

Marie-Anne did not seem at all affected by her recent flagellation and was absorbed only by present caresses. She said:

'Hold up your skirt so I can see your ass.'

I lifted my dress, a little embarrassed.

'I'm not happy with my rear. I think it's a little too fat.'

Marie-Anne contemplated it with a pensive expression as if she were measuring it.

'Your ass is very beautiful, I assure you. To prove it to you I'll kiss it.'

She placed a tender kiss on one of my round buttocks. In response, I lifted her dress and placed a kiss on her burning bottom where I could still see the marks from her recent beating. Then Marie-Anne slid her hands behind my neck and, lifting my face, kissed me on the mouth. Her tongue ran over my neck, then descended into the opening of my blouse.

I gently released myself from her and murmured:

'Let's get undressed.'

She took her clothes off first. Her body was like a Greek statue and was covered with the marks left from the Black Mass. But those multicolored tracks augmented the strange attraction of her anatomy.

'You're marvelous,' I said.

I could admire the impeccable lines of her ass, of her legs, the outline of her cunt set off by her skin, which gave her the appearance of a woman made out of a new material. Suddenly, perhaps seeing where my

47

eyes were fixed, she seized her own tits and held them out to me.

'Perhaps you like them the same way men do.'

'Yes, they're so beautiful!'

'Why that's extraordinary,' she cried. 'You like women. That's wonderful!'

Then, turning to her lover, she said:

'You understand, she likes women. We'll both lie down together and make love. She's so sweet, I want to possess her.'

I went over to her to caress her. She walked around me, looking at my tits, my abdomen, and my cunt. Then she said:

'We are equally beautiful, aren't we? Oh, how madly we're going to be able to make love! Look, George look at our two bodies.'

While talking, she had seized me by the waist and her tits were rubbing against mine. My nipples were already erect. Suddenly I wanted to feel her furry pussy around my mouth and I knelt down so that my head would be between her legs. I gently parted her vaginal lips and penetrated her with my tongue.

'I want you to lick me,' she whispered. 'You're so beautiful . . . suck me harder. I want to come this way. Bite me even harder, please! Wait, you're exciting me too much. I don't want to come yet. I want to feel your caress a little longer.'

I got up and we held each other in a voluptuous kiss. Our tongues intertwined and went deep into each other's throats.

'Press yourself against me,' she whispered, her eyes burning with a new flame.

The harder I pressed, the more excited she became, pushing herself against my naked body. Suddenly, she asked me almost maliciously:

'Tell me, have you loved other women before me? Tell me please!'

I nodded and she immediately leaned over and bit my breast violently which made me cry out in pain. Suddenly realizing that she had hurt me, she threw herself against me and began licking my body from head to toe, lingering over my cunt. Then we rolled onto the floor and embraced, sucking each other until our orgasms left us inert.

During this time, Mr Legros had not moved from his chair. But if his body had remained immobile, his eyes, on the contrary, had changed and were now veiled with lust. While we were stretched out on the carpet, he came over to Marie-Anne and began to caress her.

'Now I want you to make your lover come again,' he whispered. 'She's so beautiful when she discharges that I want to see it again.'

'Making her come is easy,' she replied.

'What's even better is that as soon as I see her about to discharge, I also want to make it. And at this rate, I'll kill myself!'

'While I open her buttocks, I want you to lick her asshole,' he suddenly demanded.

Marie-Anne instantly got on her knees between my legs and while Mr Legros enlarged the opening of my ass, the young woman's tongue penetrated me. Then he got between Marie-Anne's legs and hit her ass wildly, ordering me to turn toward him with my ass up so that while beating his mistress he could also hit me. Then he told Marie-Anne to stand up while I sucked her from behind. These various positions that we took with almost sadistic pleasure excited us tremendously, especially my partner, who was so sensitive to such erotic movements.

Then Mr Legros decided to lick Marie-Anne's ass while I rubbed his prick. I did so, but instead of manipulating his cock, I began to suck it. While I ran my tongue over him, he caressed my shoulders. His cock was so stiff by then that it hurt my lips. I felt that he was on the verge of coming when he asked us to rub each other at the same time. While my fingers sought Marie-Anne's slit, she caressed my clitoris. We both rolled on the floor, moaning with pleasure. Mr Legros was holding his cock between his fingers and pointing it at us. He asked us to suck him so he could discharge. Then suddenly he threw himself on me and pushed his enormous member into my cunt. It wasn't long before he came and a flood of sperm inundated me. When I saw that Marie-Anne was also discharging, I began writhing again, crying:

'Oh, it's good! I'm coming! I'm coming!'

CHAPTER IV
The Love Tonics

I noticed that Mr Legros discharged quite often for a man his age. When I asked him how he did it, he admitted, half amused, half embarrassed that he used aphrodisiacs. Having felt ample proof of their efficacy, I asked him to give me the recipes.

Many Madams in the past have sold drugs to their customers as well as to their girls to reawaken their potency, drugs which were really the girls' concoctions. Aphrodisiacs increase sexual possibilities and also the number of customers. Therefore courtesans are interested in increasing their knowledge of such drugs to extend their own business. Mr Legros told me that he had employed several types of stimulants and in the course of our successive meetings, he agreed to instruct me in their use. I took notes, which I then put together in a kind of manuscript. When I reread them recently, I thought that they might be interesting to my readers who will profit more from this advice than from so many of the spicy stories that are sold 'under the counter.'

This chapter, therefore, contains Mr Legros' instructions about aphrodisiacs.

'Of a hundred sexual stimulants, one alone is effective although ninety would constitute an excellent business bargain.'

These words might well serve as introduction to everything I will say about the alchemy of love. First of all we must emphasize that in everything that concerns aphrodisiacs, the ignorance of a large mass of the population has always given rise to shameless exploitation of their use. The unscrupulousness of the supposed dealers has been largely aided by a moral philosophy that is based on hypocrisy.

The alchemy of love is comprised of two categories that we must distinguish. The first concerns that which is designed to excite and increase the sexual instinct; the second, that which is to awaken love in a person for another person. We can at the outset place these two categories in the realm of superstition. We cannot overly stress the necessity of distinguishing between superstition and science, between injurious and harmless remedies. By way of example, let us examine some of the strange and unusual practices to which aphrodisiacs have been put throughout history.

The most frequent and most decisive incentives for the use of aphrodisiacs have been and still are: the impotence of the man, the frigidity of the woman, or the sterility of one or the other. And, there is another category of individuals, belonging for the most part to the privileged social classes, where idleness and debauchery has ended up in dulling the senses. Although possessing a normal constitution, these people seek stimulants to intensify their sensations. We should remark that in this case, the line between the use of the aphrodisiac as a medicine, and its abuse, is very easy to cross.

Among the numerous psychological motives pushing an individual to seek the help of aphrodisiacs, those concerning anxiety, inhibition, and fear are the most commonplace, and it is precisely the frequency with which these debilitating neuroses arise that guarantees dependence upon, and an almost superstitious belief in, the efficacy of restorative drugs and potions. It is enough to leaf through a few novels to find analyzed in great detail the state of a poor lover's soul, when he is finally given the chance to approach the one he has so long desired to fuck – and suddenly finds himself impotent because of the height and degree of his happiness.

In antiquity and in the Middle Ages, the use of aphrodisiacs was often justified by dominant religious orders. Thus we discover the old belief prevalent among the Orientals, that during fucking, bad spirits – the 'Djinns' – try to get into the cunt with the intention not only of interrupting the coitus, but also of attacking the embryo. In order to avoid this demoniacal intervention, the Orientals appealed to various means whose roles were, magical and symbolic, as well as aphrodisiacal. Omar Halevy, for example, recommended beginning the act of intercourse with a prayer and pronouncing the name of Allah at the moment of ejaculation. It was also he who prescribed the use of aphrodisiacs to Mohammed, the founder of Islam.

'We must not forget either the human condition of the prophet, the fatigues that his activities bring, nor the temptations to which he is constantly subjected by his numerous wives and slaves because each of them aspires naturally to the supreme honor of being fucked again and again by the emissary of God.'

Another motive for the use of sexual stimulants exists among certain peoples who strictly regulate the moment when the intercourse should take place. For example, the obligation to engage in intercourse on certain holidays.

Pedro de Villagonez, archbishop of Lima, relates that in old Peru they celebrated a holiday around the end of December, when the fruits reach maturity. First they observed a five-day fast which amounted to abstinence from red pepper and sexual activities. During this period the women and men met, completely naked, in the orchards. At a given signal, a general race began up to a distant hill. Each man who succeeded in catching a woman was obliged to perform a sexual act either in her cunt or her ass.

Jealousy is also a reason for the use of aphrodisiacs. There is a story about a jealous lover named Lucila who gave a potion to Lucretius, the author of *On the Nature of Things* so that she could be fucked by him again. It was this potion that was ultimately to kill the poet.

Certainly in modern times numerous other motives push individuals of both sexes to seek the aid of erotic stimulants, such as curiosity, the hobby of seduction, and competitive endurance records of fucking or being fucked, including the number of such acts accomplished in the course of a single night. The main objective in these endeavors is the intentional flaunting of sexual mores and rules established by any given society, rules which have as their origin outdated or outmoded beliefs, usually based in religious or superstitious hypocrisy. In modern society, these rules, more frequently than not, are opposed to the behavior trends observable at any given moment.

To this generally false attitude of our civilization concerning sexual laws is joined the custom of scoffing at those who are incapable of fulfilling their functions as lovers in a satisfactory way and of treating them as inferiors. The result is that men frequently do not dare to consult a doctor about these questions and are reduced to seek help at the hands of a charlatan. A manufacturer of 'intimate articles.'

It would, however, be false to read into this any sign of unusual decadence in our time. If, in modern life, we no longer find examples of the practices that ethnologists report were used by primitive peoples to augment their sexual development, or of the practices which history has passed down to us, as being common in other ages, neither should we assume that modern civilization is any more or less vulnerable to such practices than the past, or that mankind in general is any less concerned than before with the problems of its own sexuality.

These concerns, and the resulting attempts to solve the problems causing them, forced people to turn to superstition and magic for help. The Middle Ages best exemplified this attitude in its approach to medicine. Many of the cures originating in this period were based on one simple, and naive misconception: that from the exterior characteristics of plants, their shape and color, taste and odor, curative properties could be derived. Examples include vegetable juices, the odor of which evoked that of sperm or vaginal secretions, and plants, which in their shape and texture could be said to resemble a cock or a cunt. It was the same with animals. The fact that an animal was often hard, had a prolonged or violent period of heat, as well as specific odors, made certain animals appreciated and their genital organs used as stimulants.

One of the most popular sciences in the world of eroticism was that of the Chaldeans, who excited themselves by eating the liver or marrow of young boys. To them, the gods were responsible for the loss of one's virility. We have already seen how Lucretius paid for his practices with his life. Another Roman poet, Horatio, rewrote magical formulas in the form of verses although he himself seemed sceptical of their potency and use. In one of his poems he wrote: 'All the dreams, the magic, the phantoms and ghosts of sorcerers, as well as all the other sorcery only make me laugh!'

Love potions and incantations played a very important role in the Middle Ages. Among magical drinks, the Italian products were the most popular. They were carried from country to country by voyagers and all kinds of charlatans and magicians sold them to the crowds at fairs and market places. Incantations were always accompanied by magical formulas and magic words. For example, one would take the portrait of the beloved – or more simply, a piece of modeled wax which was supposed to represent that person – and heat it until it melted. Thus the person symbolized by the wax figure would be awakened to love. All these practices were attributed to diabolical inspiration and arose from black magic which was the opposite of the white magic of 'divine nature.'

The superstitions of the Middle Ages concerning sexual life even manifested themselves in the religious penal laws. An inestimable document is furnished to us by the work of two scholars, Jacob Sprenger and Heinrich Institoris. In their works they seriously consider the problem of knowing whether 'sorcerers can diminish the faculty of procreation or of amorous desire.' And the authors further wonder whether 'sorcerers are capable, by diabolical means, of bewitching the cock and ultimately pulling it off the body.'

It is true that the Catholic Church made an energetic struggle against all these superstitions in their various forms. However it did not succeed in stamping out the phallus cult in the Breton provinces until as late as the French revolution. Thus the veneration of 'Cherry brandy' in the city of Brest is nothing other than the remains of the phallic cult. According to De La Meuse, there is a chapel in this city with a statue that has a cock. Sterile women would come to this chapel and beat the statue of the saint in order to collect a little powder which they then mixed with spring water and swallowed. This statue was naked, with an erect cock which had to be restored often, due to its extensive use.

Cambry relates that in Brittany, after mass, the women had the dust in the chapel gathered up to blow on the men. They believed that by this they would seduce the heart of their beloved. In the same way, a current custom recommends the burning of sacred images so that the cinders can be added to food. In certain rigorously Catholic regions this custom has been preserved to this day.

Among these bizarre practices, one finds some which are particularly amusing. Take, for example, those whose recipes recommend swallowing a potion that is first placed in intimate contact with the desired person's sexual parts. In the Middle Ages a popular belief was that the ingestion of an apple impregnated with the sweat from the partner's armpit augmented amorous passion. Another superstition attributed aphrodisiacal properties to certain shells which had first been in the desired person's digestive tract and removed from his excrement.

What hasn't man done to obey the god of love! He has allowed himself to be burned, marked, painted, tattooed, has had recourse to the strangest manipulations, to the most complicated formulas – without so much as wondering if there really was a causal relationship between the means employed and the resulting sexual activity.

It is again in the category of superstitions that we must class the talismans and amulets whose principal ingredients are, even today, blood, hair, pubic hairs, skin, and human nails. Most of the time, the phenomenon of autosuggestion is involved here. It is not the amulette itself but the faith in its efficacy which sometimes produces the desired effect. Even today certain men only have to tell themselves: 'I am excited, therefore I am hard, therefore I am capable of fucking' to see their cocks swell up, take on considerable dimensions, and be ready to fuck.

As for some women, they only have to

imagine a beautiful, well sculptured cock with taut veins, puffed out prettily, with heavy balls and nice hairs between vigorous thighs to get more aroused than if they had recited several incantations with incomprehensible words. Moreover, the strange words must have permitted their thoughts to wander to more stimulating ideas rather than having any meaning themselves.

It is the same for the erotic action of certain precious stones. During the Middle Ages, people strongly believed in the influence that precious stones were supposed to exercise on their bearers. We know, for example, that as early as antiquity, when Cleopatra made a pearl dissolve in vinegar, she was less guided by prodigality than by the desire to increase the sensitivity of her admirable cunt.

Even today you can hear talk of the supernatural virtues of the ruby which is supposed to facilitate the success of amorous desires and assure in addition the richness and happiness of its wearer. The moonstone, for example, also passes as a treasure which not only conserves one's moral purity but also love and fidelity. Belief in the extraordinary power of precious stones has always been closely tied to the idea that the action of the precious stone was influenced by the course of the stars.

*   *   *

Now I want to tell you about those aphrodisiacs whose value has been recognized by modern science and which, consequently, deserve a particular interest.

It is a notorious fact that certain products exercise an undeniable influence on the sexual faculties. In certain cases, the quantity and quality of the food can determine the state of the cock and balls. Vitamins play an important role in this regard. It is interesting to know that numerous scientists have demonstrated the influence of Vitamin E. It appears that among rats nourished steadily on Vitamin E, the genital organs develop in extraordinary proportion to the rest of the body and the mating period stretches out over the whole year, even among the weak specimens whose weight at the time of puberty is as much as a third of normal weight.

There are two ways of augmenting the deposit of vitamins in the organism: by observing a diet in which preference is given to foods rich in vitamins and by instituting a cure of special medicines containing vitamins in a concentrated state which the modern pharmacy puts within reach of all of us.

This afternoon, after becoming aroused, Mr Legros tied a strange object to his cock which increased its volume and augmented his sexual strength. Fucked by a prick developed by artificial means, I enjoyed a strange new pleasure. After discharging, Mr Legros gave me the following explanations which I hastened to write down so I wouldn't forget.

The goal of genital deformation in man is not to augment the sensitivity of the male but that of the female. For the most part, it concerns surgical enlargement of the cock. There are also accessories that one can attach exteriorly to the member without resorting to an operation. To this category belongs the 'guesquel' of the Indians of Patagonia. This is a sort of ring of mule hair attached by a string to the gland in such a way that the hairs are held forward. The scientist Stoll gives the following description:

'In the beginning the Indians did not enjoy the guesquel much because it caused them pain and even light hemorrhages, but gradually they became accustomed to its use, even in their conjugal lives. The Indians of Patagonia are distinguished by their slightly frigid temperament which means that the Indians prefer white women when they can get them. They think that the white women are more exciting and behave in a more active manner during the sexual act, which they like very much. They call them "crocoveadores," which means "creatures who make grimaces and move around." In order to provoke a more active attitude in their own women, the Indians use the "guesquel." The effect of this is so powerful that the women utter cries during the sexual act and their orgasm is so intense that they are left completely exhausted. The use of the guesquel does not seem to bring about any special inconveniences. A well made guesquel brings very high prices. It is often worth as much as two horses!'

In Java you find similar devices. The natives attach a piece of goat skin to their cocks before coitus. Another method, widespread among the Battas in Sumatra, is much less inoffensive. They practise an incision on the gland and introduce stones, shells, or gold or silver balls under the skin. When the incision is closed, the penis is all puffed up due to these foreign bodies.

But it is the 'ampallangs' of the Dayak tribes of Borneo which are monstrous. The gland, after having been flattened between two bamboo boards for several days, is pierced by a bamboo stalk. The canal thus dug is destined to receive a pigeon feather – which the man never removes – in order to prevent the closing up of the canal. Only before intercourse, is the feather replaced by the ampallang. Here is how Miklusho-Maclay describes this custom:

'During work and on his trips, the Dayak

keeps a feather in the canal. At the moment of sexual intercourse the feather is replaced by the ampallang which consists of a piece of leather, silver, or gold, four centimeters long and two millimeters thick. One of the extremities is terminated by a ball of hard metal. A second ball is tied to the other extremity of the ampallang, once the apparatus is put into place. We also find ampallangs whose balls turn around the cock. The whole apparatus reaches from five to ten centimeters in length.

'The women have the right to order the ampallang. When the husband refuses to use it his wife can demand a divorce. Once accustomed to this device, the women can no longer do without it. During the sexual act the men introduce the ampallang obliquely into the woman's organ.'

Other devices of the same type are utilized by a great number of primitive peoples. Lindshoten, for example, describes an apparatus that the Peruvians wear, which is passed into the penis and whose construction is similar to that of the ampallang, with the distinction that the balls are replaced by small bells. Another method which is not, however, destined directly to produce mechanical sexual excitation, is the tatooing that is practiced in various forms and on all parts of the bodies of both sexes.

*   *   *

Mr Legros told me about many artificial erotic
devices on other occasions. But I didn't keep
any notes other than the ones I have reported
here.

CHAPTER V
Fresh Love

I did not sleep with customers just for money, but also with people I liked for my own pleasure. When I think about that period of my life during which I visited Marie-Anne and Mr Legros frequently, one day stands out in my memory. I don't exactly know why it was so special. Perhaps its charm will come out as I tell the events of that day.

The sun had just awakened me. A ray played on my hair and disturbed the beautiful dream I was having. I was being kissed by Jack. It was very sweet, very pleasant, and the dream would probably have lasted a long time. That ray of sunlight was very indiscreet to disturb my voluptuous dream.

I smiled and readied myself to come back to reality. It wasn't enough to dream; one has to live. It's true that it was a Sunday and that, for me, Sunday meant a return to life, but it also meant a return to dreaming. There were three dreams possible to me, three dreams with three different heroes. I could dream of Jean Maurice, or of Max.

Jean had invited me to go for a car ride at noon, to have lunch in the country at a little inn where the food was delicious, and where we could take a walk after lunch or dance and listen to the music of the strolling singers. That was a very tempting proposition. I loved to eat good food and I knew that Jean was a connoisseur and would take me to a good restaurant.

Maurice had also asked me out. But he didn't have a car. We would take the train and go to the seaside where we would eat fried food on the beach and then go boating. This prospect was also a pleasing one. It was a beautiful day and it would be charming to be by the water.

Which would I choose? The car or the boat? Both were charming. Jean was a great boy, full of gaity and intelligence. And he was such a good dancer. I was never bored with him. Maurice was very sentimental. He knew all the right witty and poetic words to say while the boat was gliding through the water. But how could I forget Max? He loved the peaceful, Parisian pleasures and had offered to take me to the races, then to dine in a nice restaurant and later to spend the evening at the theater.

I hadn't promised any of my three knights yet. I had told them I would call before eleven if I was going to accept their invitation. Soon I would get dressed and go down to that nice tenant on the third floor who would let me use her telephone.

It was quite a difficult choice. I intended to enjoy every minute of my Sunday. Whom should I favor with my company? I wanted this day to be perfect. Which of the three would be the most skillful lover? Who seemed to be the most in love with me, the most sincere, the most devoted, the least egotistical? Which of the three would be just as interested in the pleasure he gave to his lover as he was in his own pleasure?

All these questions were very troubling and there were moments when I thought it would be much simpler not to have to choose at all, but to abandon myself to the great laws of chance and to entrust myself to Cupid. If I had to choose and the day did not turn out just right, then I would regret not having chosen Jean rather than Max, or Maurice rather than Jean.

Suddenly I thought of the conversation I had had with one of my friends who was much more experienced than I and who had said:

'If you are hesitating between your three suitors and if you wonder which of the three to choose, it's because you don't love any of them. If you loved one of the three you wouldn't hesitate a second nor would you even consider the other two.'

I thought about it and realized that my friend was right. I liked all three boys but I hadn't yet felt that strange, mysterious evil called Love. Suddenly I decided that I might as well just toss a coin. Perhaps chance really would be the best judge.

I seized a coin and cried:

'First, between Jean and Maurice . . . Heads it's Jean tails it's Maurice.' Maurice won. 'Now between Maurice and Max . . . Heads it's Max, tails it's Maurice.'

The coin rolled onto the ground and before I could see which side was up, the doorbell rang. This was strange because I wasn't expecting anyone at that hour.

'Open up, Svetlana, it's me, Jack!'

'What, you? You're back?'

'Of course, open the door!'

I was so surprised that I was breathless. I threw on a robe and let my unexpected visitor come in. He hadn't even bothered to call me first. He took me in his arms and put me down on the bed in the sunlight.

'My little Svetlana,' he cried. 'How happy I am to see you again. It's been over a year since I left! But you're even prettier than before!'

Then he kissed me – on the face, on the mouth, on the ears. I was experiencing the same joy that he was and I manifested my satisfaction with several sighs and little cries of pleasure. I no longer wondered whether I was capable of loving, because I was too busy enjoying this treat that was being offered. There was no longer any question of having lunch at an inn, of dancing, of listening to music, of having fried food on the water or of going boating. No more thought of going to the races or the theater. It was going to be an evening of love and sensuality. I had no more will power. Jack was already stretching me out on the bed. I knew what was going to happen and I did nothing to prevent it.

While he was covering my face with passionate kisses he took off my robe. His eyes filled with ecstasy when he saw my body and he seized one of my nipples in his mouth and bit it playfully. I was already trembling in his arms. I removed the rest of my clothes myself, and arched my chest toward him because I wanted him to go on biting me. I trembled at the touch of his lips. At first he only caressed me lightly. He ran his hands over my skin and fondled my breasts at great length. Then, almost savagely, he grabbed them and pinched them, digging his nails in like a baker pinching bread. I uttered unconscious little moans because his caresses were so good. Then, sliding my nipple between his thumb and index finger, he began to rub it, which excited me even more. My nipples were hard with excitement and I was beginning to moan loudly. In an uncontrollable movement, I seized the young man's head and pressed it against my torso. Jack understood my desire and ran his tongue over my body, drawing deep moans from me again. His kisses became more erotic. At times his mouth would completely absorb one of my breasts and I had the impression that he was going to tear it off. Under his caresses my desire augmented and I asked him to suck me lower. He obeyed and his tongue licked my nudity untiringly, stopping on my neck, then descending insidiously toward my navel. My young lover's caresses were driving me mad and I couldn't control myself. In a nervous gesture, I removed the only remaining thing I had on − a tiny triangle of black lace. Then I arched my back and offered him my cunt. Jack was surprised by my movement but his desire was so great that he leaned forward and ran his tongue around my cunt, exciting me terribly. He licked the border of my hole, advanced a little, but just at the opening went back to my abdomen. His little game was making me sick with desire and I was writhing with lust. My thighs parted and Jack got on his knees between them. I saw his enormously stiff cock between my legs. I leaned forward and brought his dilated member up to my slit. It felt so good that I let out a cry of delight.

My companion's eyes were burning with desire. He seized his cock and placed it in my cunt. I sighed with ecstasy and grabbed his hand as if to thank him for what he had done. He stretched out next to me and lowered himself completely. I pressed myself against him and his warmth made me tremble. He was covered with sweat and I could feel his chest panting against mine. His fingers caressed my thighs, my ass, and my asshole, which sent shivers down my spine.

He held my face in his hands and kissed me from time to time. Our tongues sought each other and we seemed to be trying to swallow one another.

Then I felt Jack's hand playing at the entrance to my cunt, and finally one of his fingers moved inside me. I tightened my thighs around him and imprisoned his finger inside me. Then I released my legs so that he could continue his exploration. Suddenly he withdrew his finger and, adjusting his cock against my cunt, he introduced it gently. I moaned with joy as I felt his enormous rod slipping into me. I began to move so that I could feel the penetration better. I was no longer in control of myself. I threw my head back and almost screamed:

'At last! It's marvelous, my love, you're fucking me, it's marvelous!'

I was moving under my young lover and I felt an extraordinary exaltation rising within me. I wanted to kiss him and I forced my tongue inside his mouth. Then a wave of passion submerged me and I let out a great cry of pleasure.

The whole day was filled with such memories. Jack fucked me eight times that Sunday.

CHAPTER VI
Adorable Yolande

But even though I loved men, I loved women just as much. The human animal is omnivorous – he feeds off everything. I didn't have to stop at a single sex like the poor limited creatures who are incapable of tasting the diversity of the joys of this world.

Yolande was young and beautiful. The day I met her she had decided to assuage her long-suppressed desires and offer herself to some woman of little virtue of whom she had dreamed for so long. A lesbian terrified by her own erotic nature, she had resisted her desires until the moment when their intensity had pushed her into the street in search of a person capable of satisfying her. Chance threw us together.

She looked at me in such a way that I would have had to be blind not to understand. I smiled at her, acquiescent.

She stood still and waited for me. I went over to her.

'How beautiful you are,' murmured Yolande.

'So are you, my dear.'

I wasn't lying. She had an adorable tall and slender body with delicate curves. Her adolescent face with its green eyes, perfect mouth, and shiny white teeth inspired admiration by its harmony and naive candor.

'How much do you want to make love with me?' asked Yolande cynically.

'I have a set fee,' I answered. 'But since you are appealing to me, you will have the right to some additional treats for the same price.'

She was intelligent and understood quickly.

'Thank you.'

She followed me.

In the hotel room I undressed and offered myself to her, preoccupied with her pleasure. She was avid with desire and thirsty for erotic caresses. She discharged very quickly with a cry of happiness. Then I concerned myself with my own desires.

I ordered her to walk around the room as she was, totally naked, and I didn't even try to touch her. She immediately did as I asked, slid out of bed, and began to walk. She must have felt my eyes resting on her breasts that were still stiff with excitement, on her ass, her legs, everything that excited me so. She lifted her arms and moved her abdomen within reach of my mouth and my passionate hands. Then she turned away quickly without inhibitions or false modesty. Offering the spectacle of that flesh, Yolande suddenly felt herself bathed in all the ferments of shame. She came back to me, leaned over, then half opened her lips for a burning kiss that made her body undulate and increased my desire. She moaned softly, letting herself be carried away again by the wave of strange sensations that was making the blood vessels in her temples stand out.

There was a flame burning in my eyes as I lifted her effortlessly. Then she came to me, completely naturally, while I dug my fingers into her shoulders, then into her ass.

Yolande held back a cry, exhaled painfully, and sighed. I loved the pain I was inflicting upon her and it excited me more. Now I knew that I could do with Yolande as I wished. She trembled when I bit her on the neck, and lay still under the violent pain I was inflicting upon her cunt, the pain that was breaking her completely. With a child-like gesture, she put her teeth on her own hand to keep from screaming. Then she accompanied me with her whole body in a pleasure that had increased tenfold, that made her pant and brought passionate words to her lips.

Then Yolande fell back and a flood of secretions spread out in her burning cunt. She could not restrain herself any longer and in a single outburst, expressed the sum of pains and pleasures, new sensations and built-up dreams which had been bound up within her until now.

I sought her mouth softly and only finding her cheek in the semi-darkness of that thick hair, I kissed her. Perfectly lucid, Yolande soon realized that I was going to leave her. Then she was alone – but not for long. In the dark she sensed a silhouette moving near her, stretching out next to her and touching her. She held her breath, afraid to turn around, waiting . . .

I touched her skin but remained silent. Yolande was still, trembling. I did not speak. We were, after all, there for action.

Then it began again. I took her hand and placed it against my cunt so she could become acquainted with it. She did not oppose me in any way. I began to renew all of my sexual memories. She gave me her body which I bent to my fantasies. Her body was a plaything in my passionate hands. I used it in my way – wordlessly. I caressed her wildly. She didn't dare look at me. I grabbed her ankles and raised her legs, then I pushed a godemiche into her. I wanted to make her scream with happiness. The need to irritate her delicate satiny skin made me pull her violently. Everything in me was confused – my desire to make her suffer and to give her pleasure.

Actually Yolande was suffering and she could no longer keep from crying out in pain. She did not know where she was or whether what remained of her mind would irrevocably be destroyed in the shock. She felt her entire body breaking into little pieces, and suddenly she let out a sharp cry that sprang from her very depths.

I continued my efforts despite everything without worrying about what she was thinking or feeling. She must have lost her concept of time just as I did. She attached her claws to me, planting her nails in my shoulders, my chest. She must have thought I had no compassion because I did not give her any respite. Captive of my desires, she had to submit. But all that was nothing compared to what followed. I pushed her on to the end of her strength and resources, and she followed me. I knew that she was going to burst and dissolve around me. I pursued my way without worrying about her. I took her out of herself again as she writhed, conquered without daring to ask for mercy, with the strange need inside her to go on farther, always farther . . . to pull the ultimate desire and the final hunk of sexual potential from her body!

Yolande was in agony. Her eyes were wild, her brain delirious, and she was babbling frantically without knowing a word she was saying. She contracted completely in a movement of total abandon and also of defense as if to repulse her inhuman assailant.

She uttered a tearing cry and began to literally melt in my arms, broken, panting, dying, fainting, losing her footing in that fathomless pit into which she had plunged – happy, superbly reawakened, avenged, all her veins pumping furiously in search of her finally realized desires.

CHAPTER VII
The Actress-Whore

Then Anne-Luce came into my life.

At the time I met her she was at the height of her artistic and amorous glory. All of Paris was at her feet, if not between her thighs.

But first I would like to describe her and furnish several important details of her strange biography.

October 2, 19— witnessed the debut of a young actress of sixteen, named Anne-Luce. Her beautiful oval face, her adorable fresh complexion, her big, brown eyes and abundant, silky chestnut hair immediately charmed the audiences at the Théâtre Francaise. Not only was Miss Luce delicious to look at, but she acted with great feeling and style.

'There is a perfect young woman,' whispered many of the spectators.

Like many other actresses, Anne-Luce was born in the wings. Her father and mother

were with the Comédie Francaise, he as a
musician and she as a costumer. Little Anne
was brought up hearing talk all around her
of plays, roles, etc. So she naturally
developed a passion for the theater.

After her first success as an actress she felt
another vocation being awakened in her.

'Who will pick that fresh flower?' many
men would wonder, astounded and
entranced by Anne's virginly grace. In order
to find out, some of them showed up at the
young actress' dressing room and began to
court her. In her beautiful dressing gown with
her bosom exposed, Miss Luce listened to all
the compliments, even the most daring,
smiled, and did not discourage anyone.

To herself, Anne wondered:

'Who should I take as a lover?'

Cold-blooded despite her youthful
appearance, the young actress felt the soul
of a courtesan awakening in her. Far from
being revolted by the most audacious
propositions, the clearest offers, the
increasing liberties that her visitors took with
her, Anne behaved seductively with them all.
Finally, when a rich businessman from
Hamburg named Frank whispered in her ear
while caressing her, 'Dearest, won't you come
to my hotel tomorrow,' the young virgin
answered softly with an angelic smile, 'why
not? I'll leave everything up to you.'

'Don't be afraid. You won't regret it.'
Miss Luce answered with a smile.

At the appointed hour, Anne arrived at their rendezvous. She was thinking only of surrendering to Frank's desires. But Frank was still young and had a very gentle nature. His caresses and kisses disturbed her deliciously. A sweet languor invaded her. A violent desire took hold of her entire being, as Frank ran his impatient hands over her body. Then he lifted her blouse with a quick gesture.

The young girl's two globes appeared before the man's adoring eyes. Then to his delight, she began to undress herself quietly, almost timidly. Her body was totally naked before him now. She arched her back, waiting to be kissed. The man caressed her with skillful fingers, and she was ready to succumb to him. Frank ran his hands over her chest, barely touching her at first, then, grabbing her breasts gently, he caressed them between his fingers. The young girl uttered unconscious moans. The man rubbed her nipples which were stiff with excitement. Perhaps still unconsciously she seized the man's head and drew it to her. Frank's lips half opened to taste the skin that was so deliciously offered. Now he began licking her entire body. His mouth opened and he took one of her breasts, enclosing it completely between his lips.

Under this skillful handling, the young girl became very excited and begged him to continue kissing her. His mouth ran over her naked skin and his tongue was untiring in its licking of the most intimate corners of her body. He moved to her neck, descended over her breasts, her stomach, and then stopped only because the young girl still had her panties on.

Frank's caresses had excited her terribly and she could no longer control herself. She offered him her entire body. Encouraged by her moans, he lifted the elastic of her panties and admired her thighs which were already separated. He gently removed the tiny garment and, with eyes burning with desire, he contemplated her pussy.

The young girl was still. The man stretched out next to her and then got on his knees between her legs. He took out his cock, swollen with desire, and placed it over Anne's vaginal lips as she moaned with ecstasy. Trembling with emotion and desire, the adolescent brought her hand down to her partner. The man had undressed completely and the young girl felt her chest against his virile torso. Pressing herself to him, she kissed his chest. Frank caressed her and touched her ass. Then he held the young girl's face in his hands and they were united in a passionate kiss. Frank moved his hand slowly toward that cunt that had never been penetrated.

The man reached her silky down and with infinite precaution slid a finger inside her. The girl wanted to feel his caresses more deeply and she separated her thighs in order to open herself to the embrace she desired secretly in her heart and body.

The man's fingers advanced further into her cunt. Then he got up, grabbed his cock that was enormous now, and placed it against her hole. He tried to penetrate very gently and seeing that he was already a little way in, he pushed himself all the way with a single blow. The girl screamed and writhed. She sought Frank's mouth and her tongue found his; her sighs of pain were transformed into gasps of pleasure.

Anne was no longer in control of herself. Her legs were parting more and more while in a rhythmical movement, Frank fucked her continually. He arched his back and she fell back, uttering a plaintive cry of ecstasy. At the same instant, her lover discharged, exalted by the act he had just committed.

She had given herself so well that, nine months later, she brought a beautiful little girl into the world.

Wild with joy, Frank, who believed he was Anne's only lover, gave the child ten million francs. It wasn't long, however, before he realized that her virtue was very unsteady.

While Anne-Luce was watching her success in the theater increase and her reputation as a woman grow, the war broke out. Like many other actresses she helped the soldiers know the joys of the home front.

In 1919 she started her own theater. Then began a period of new triumphs for the young actress-courtesan. Ann-Luce owned a very beautiful hotel on St George Street that was richly furnished. Everyone whose pockets were full enough immediately ran to the ex-ingenue to admire her beauty, and to try their luck with her. But all these interested visitors, all these impatient lovers first had to reckon with Rose, Anne-Luce's servant. This domestic was charged with the defense of her mistress' interests. It was she who received the men who were rich enough to aspire to Anne's charms. Here is how a friend of mine depicted Rose's method:

'She asks only for money but it is a trap. If one gives without counting, he is considered a charming man. If he counts, he is thrown out . . . they say that Rose modestly only gets ten percent commission. Once the visitor has appeased the watchdog with cash or a check, he is finally admitted to see the mistress of the house. She receives him dressed in an open tunic under which the charming actress is half-naked.'

I also heard a very funny story about Anne-

Luce. It seems that a rich man named Serge decided that he wanted her to become his mistress. With this goal in mind, he went to one of his friends and said:

'I would like to offer Anne-Luce a car. Only it seems to me more delicate not to take it to her myself! What do you think?'

In a polite and indifferent tone, the friend responded:

'Well it seems more gallant that way.'

'Wonderful! In that case, would you be the one to offer the car in my name?'

Serge's friend hesitated, then smiled maliciously and declared:

'My friend, you can count on me! Tomorrow Anne-Luce will be in possession of your beautiful gift.'

He kept his word. The following day he presented himself at the actress' home, showed her the man's superb gift, and said:

'My darling, permit me to offer you this car in homage to your beauty.'

The delighted Miss Luce exclaimed:

'Why, you overwhelm me! I don't know how to express my gratitude.'

Serge's friend took her hand and kissed it, then drawing the young woman into his arms, he murmured:

'Are you sure?'

Anne smiled and offered her lips to the man she took to be a very generous lover.

'You know, the most beautiful girl in the world can only give what she has.'

'What more could anyone ask?' cried the visitor with a satisfied grin. Then he impatiently led her into her bedroom.

Anne approached the man and drew him over to the bed. She bent down and pressed her head against her friend's neck. He kissed her on the cheek and then descended to the opening in her blouse. There he placed his lips on her chest. She moved her sensual mouth to her partner's face. Then he felt Anne's hand slowly unbuttoning his pants as she continued to kiss him. She did not completely undo them but contented herself with taking his rod out. Then she licked his chest, descended very slowly toward his navel. She stopped there and finally reached for his cock again. Her white teeth took hold of the burning flesh and she began to bite her companion's throbbing gland, and move her head back and forth between the man's thighs. The contact of the woman's tongue no doubt became more and more exciting, for the man's cock was unbelievably stiff. His eyes had become clouded. Her lips were open now, and the man was writhing as if he could no longer stand the agony. Suddenly the woman's mouth filled with a viscous liquid and the man's rod was emptied by several irregular jolts that shook his entire body.

Although he might have preferred to rest, he thought he owed the woman some gratitude. He removed her pale, satin dress and began to embrace her passionately. First he caressed her cunt with the tips of his fingers. Soon she began to murmur:

'My love, you have excited me terribly. Come, fuck me . . .'

He obeyed, but not being stiff yet, he leaned between Anne's thighs and his expert tongue moved inside her. He bit her vaginal lips and rubbed her gently, then moved his hand like a cock in a measured rhythm. Anne was moaning and writhing. Then she cried out and fell back on the bed while her lover, who was excited again, continued to suck her cunt.

While Anne tried to regain her breath, the man asked:

'May I take you again?'

She smiled at him, happy to see her partner appreciating the charms of her body. He saw that the actress was willing so he began to caress her again. Soon she said:

'Come, my love . . . now I want you to take me. I'm yours, come!'

Anne was panting with desire. Her body was writhing, her breasts were erect, and she drew the man against her naked body, pressing her abdomen against his stiff cock and crying:

'I want you, my love. Come, fuck me! Make me know your body. Be quick, darling!' With a quick movement, he was on top of her, feeling her burning breasts on his chest.

Anne seized the man's member and pushed it into her cunt.

'Come, darling, fuck me now. Harder! Harder!

Wild with pleasure, the man balled her passionately and they both lost themselves in the intoxication of their lovemaking.

The next day, Serge, with a conquering smile on his lips, presented himself at the actress' house and asked Anne whether she liked the car.

'I don't understand. The car was yours?'

The man was quite surprised to learn how his commission had been carried out. The conclusion of the scene? As Serge's friend, who was later to become my lover told me, Anne-Luce was made to pay twice! The rich Serge obtained what he wanted, and Anne-Luce became his mistress from then on.

However, Frank, the man who had been Anne's first lover, and was the father of her child, brought his affair before the courts and ordered the return of the financial settlement he had made on the child. He lost the case. That same evening, the charming actress put on a comedy at her theater. In the play, one of the characters acquired proof that his mistress had deceived him. Anne-Luce played the role. With a wild air, the actress shouted:

'What are you asking me? Speak up. What do I owe you?'

'The money you got from me!'

The play caused a sensation; the whole audience laughed and applauded. From then on its success, as long as Anne-Luce played in it, was assured.

Anne-Luce also owned a theater to which people came to watch lewd plays performed with naked actresses. Now Anne, who, as we have seen, had a good business sense, soon realized that she could add a supplementary business which would finish what the first business began so well. Therefore, she financed a house that became famous throughout Paris, all the more so because she participated not only as a manager but also as an employee.

I went to Anne-Luce's brothel one night, when it was at the height of its fame. I was accompanied by Alice, a young girl from a good family with an admirable body and a passionate nature who had just tasted the pleasures of Lesbos in my company. She liked both sexes and George, one of her many lovers, accompanied us.

The house occupied almost a whole block in a wealthy section of town. Rose, Anne-Luce's servant, met us at the door. She was magnificently dressed in a very short, low-cut black lace dress. She looked us over carefully, then had us come into one of the rooms, a true old-fashioned boudoir with red drapes and a big bed, ideal for orgies.

'We would like to meet and make love with Miss Anne-Luce,' Alice declared simply.

Rose laughed.

'You come right to the point! But Miss Luce doesn't make love with just anyone. First she asks me to try people out, because if they are not sufficiently interesting, she cannot accept them into her exclusive, intimate clan.'

Then our hostess went over to Alice, and touched her face with the tips of her fingers.

'My, what soft skin you have! Very nice! You're beautiful. Please undress so I can appreciate the beauty of your body.'

Alice recoiled a little, but the servant paid no attention.

'Go on, undress!' she insisted.

Alice turned to George and asked him his opinion, although she knew his response in advance as well as she knew what she was going to do.

'Tell me, George, do I have to undress in front of this woman?'

'Why, of course, that's why we came here. Don't be ridiculous!'

With a perverted smile, the adolescent began to undress. Slowly she removed her blouse, her skirt, her slip, and finally her bra and panties, revealing two tiny tits with red nipples and her furry pussy. She rolled her stockings down her nubile legs and stood before us completely naked.

Rose walked around her, touching her breasts, her stomach, her thighs, and caressed her pussy in passing.

'You're not bad at all! No, you're even very good. You only need a few lessons to become one of the most captivating of our girls.'

Alice didn't seem to understand the servant's words, and I was a little astonished myself that it was Rose who was looking us over. I thought that the directress of the brothel was going to greet us in person. The servant explained:

'You know, I'm always the one who receives guests. When I have made my choice, I present the young person to the owner and she decides what her relationship with the client will be.

'Oh, that's all right,' I answered.

While young Alice, nude as a statue, but adorably alive, turned slowly among us so we could admire her charms, Rose came over to me and, pressing herself against me, murmured:

'You must know that you are also very beautiful. Your body would drive me wild if I could hold you in my arms.'

I looked into her eyes without answering, vaguely excited myself. Then Rose turned to George:

'You undress too.'

Our companion smiled and began to remove his shirt, his pants, his shoes and socks, and finally his shorts. Then he stood naked before us. Rose, who seemed capable of being everywhere at the same time, was not insensitive to the male physique.

'You have the body of an athlete,' she said. 'You are very exciting.'

And then she looked at all three of us:

'Now I am going to undress!'

I felt a little pull on my heart when I heard these words because from the instant I had set my eyes on her, I had had a wild desire to see her anatomy in detail. She didn't take long to remove her dress and slide it to her feet. Then I saw her naked for the first time. I shivered. I liked her body more than I could have dreamed. She had splendid shoulders, highly perched breasts that were white and large, a marble stomach, and – what surprised me the most in this girl – a tiny cunt in comparison to her long thighs. Her pussy was only a miniscule point bordered by fur.

She was much too experienced not to guess that she excited me considerably. Yet, she did not come to me, but went to George, instead.

She seized his cock and our friend's prick soon took on engaging proportions between her long skillful fingers. While she caressed George, she never took her eyes off me.

'Don't you want to undress?' she asked, visibly excited.

I was the only person in the room still dressed.

'You don't like me, do you? Tell me! Come over here and caress me. Wouldn't you like to put your beautiful tongue into my sticky little cunt?'

I couldn't resist the vulgarity of those words and undressed with nervous movements. Rose kept her eyes glued to me. She uttered a sigh of satisfaction when she saw me naked:

'You're lovely,' she said.

I went over to her body that was hypnotizing me and, getting down on my knees, I took her cunt between my trembling lips. She moaned softly, which excited me even more. First I licked the hairy contour of her cunt and then pushed my tongue into the depths of her vagina. While I was sucking her, one of my hands played with her hairs, and the other caressed her breasts.

Rose, however, was still caressing George whose hand was foraging in Alice's pussy. The maid was writhing and murmuring passionate words which excited me more.

'Oh, how well you fuck! Your tongue is

going so far into me! Oh, it's so good. Lick me harder, you whore! I love this! Oh, pinch my hairs, pull them out. Suck me again, deeper.'

Then suddenly she changed her tone and shouted:

'I can never come like this! You'll have to use a dildo. There are several in that drawer over there . . .'

The drawer that Rose had indicated contained a veritable collection of false cocks. I chose the largest and the longest and tied it round my waist. Then I went back to Rose and, caressing her a little first with my finger, I penetrated her quickly with my enormous prick. While I fucked her, she continued to massage George with increased pressure, as he continued to occupy himself with Alice.

Then suddenly I felt a hand on my ass. I noticed that the arm belonged to George. I liked this very much and, excited by Alice's tearing cries, as well as by Rose's encouragement, I soon discharged. My companions quickly followed me. When George was ready to come, Rose demanded him to direct the stream into her mouth and she swallowed all the sperm which, added to the intensity of my caress, made her discharge instantly.

When we had recovered, Rose called a valet and asked him to bring us refreshments. Then she declared:

'If you like I can show you what goes on in the other rooms. All our rooms are constructed in such a way that everyone can see what the other is doing. It's very exciting to watch other people make love. Come with me, you won't regret it . . .'

Completely naked, which was very pleasant on that warm summer day, we followed her. We soon found ourselves in a long, dark corridor which contained several doors. There was a tiny, hidden slit in each of them that permitted us to see what was going on inside. In one of the rooms there was a couple fucking. In another some women were caressing each other. Further on, there were men making love to each other. At the end of the corridor, there was a big door, in the middle of which was a half-open window which enlarged the field of vision considerably. A true orgy the likes of which I had never seen was taking place in that room. About ten naked men and women were sucking, fucking, or whipping one another. Bottles of champagne were spread around the floor and those that were still full were being poured into women's cunts or between their breasts, and even in their asses.

'This is one of our best clients,' Rose told us. 'She rents this room once a month and brings all her friends here.'

Rose was behind me and her breasts were

brushing my back, while I felt her cunt hairs caressing my ass. It was very pleasant.

'If you like, we can join them. They are always happy to have other guests. They are really too accustomed to one another.'

Without having to consult one another, we went eagerly into the room through a little door skillfully hidden by a thick, green velvet curtain. When we came in, no one noticed our presence. Each of the participants was too busy in some lascivious act.

We moved into the room as a splendid creature with fire-red hair approached me and held out a whip with a mother-of-pearl handle.

'You're so beautiful! Come on, beat me!'

She went over to the wall, her arms raised, her back bare and covered with bruises from past blows. With her splendid buttocks, her sculptured legs, and beautiful face, the stranger had just the kind of body that excited me very quickly. I grabbed the whip and began to beat her violently. She cried and moaned, not from pain but from passion.

'Oh, it's so good! You're beating me divinely! I can tell that you're used to it! Go on, my dear, it's marvelous. Beat my ass then go on up to my shoulders. I want you to hit me with all your might. Oh, you're exciting me. You're beautiful. Beat me even harder.

I'm going to come if you continue like this. Oh, it's so good!'

I liked punishing this creature and the words she was shouting were facilitating my work. Suddenly she turned around and arched her chest.

'No, beauty, beat me on the front! Here are my breasts. Let the lashes of your whip enter my cunt. There! Oh, that's good. Again! Deeper. Push them in deeper!'

Excited, I began to beat her with real violence, aiming at her magnificent breasts. The whip turned their immaculate marble whiteness to flaming red. The saliva was running over her chin and her face was contorted. Then she began to pant very loudly. Suddenly she fell back, crying:

'I'm coming, I'm coming, I'm coming!'

She was so exhausted by our little game that her knees bent and she crumbled to the floor.

Then I took a godemiche, put it around my waist, and still terribly excited, approached my beautiful companion. She had closed her eyes and was half unconscious. I kissed her face and covered her whole body, particularly the wounds I had caused, with passionate kisses. She looked at me and murmured:

'I'll never forget you. I love you. You were so marvelous. No man has ever given me such pleasure! I want to keep you to myself!'

101

She caressed my face with infinite care as if she was afraid of hurting me. I separated her legs gently and brought my cock to her slit. First I inserted the tip, then I penetrated her in a single blow. She moaned softly, and her eyes were ecstatic with happiness. I fucked her harder and harder, content to watch the pleasure I was giving her.

Then Rose came over to us and grabbed my hand.

'Oh, no! I'm the one who brought you here. You owe me the pleasure.'

And almost brutally she drew me to her, pulling me away from the beautiful stranger. Perhaps I was embarrassed because I didn't react, although in my heart and body I had no desire whatsoever to fuck the servant. I wanted to continue my work on the redhead. That poor woman was now looking at me with an expression of disgust. Big tears were running over her cheeks as she shouted:

'You're no better than men! It's always the latest arrival who has all the advantages. You're nothing but a whore!'

She got up and went over to a man who was alone. She put her arms around him and asked him to fuck her. The man consented but when he didn't seem to screw her hard enough, she pushed him away and started to masturbate.

As for me, Rose had succeeded in making

me penetrate her with my godemiche but I never took my eyes off my beautiful stranger. I imagined she was the one I was fucking. Rose, thanks to her own fingers, the pretty stranger, and me, came at the same moment. As soon as the maid was finished, she lifted her head and cried:

'There is Madame!'

I followed her eyes and saw Anne-Luce, the actress, whose famous face had been popularized by photographs in newspapers and on bill-boards. She was blonde with delicate cheeks, clear blue eyes, a perfect mouth, and the serious pure face of a girl deprived of all sexual thoughts. I had already had enough experience to know that this type of creature often hides an extraordinary perversity, as if eroticism had wanted to avenge itself by corrupting the soul of the person guilty of being physically too beautiful.

The mistress of the house looked at me for a few minutes, then, turning to Rose, made a sign for her to come with her. The servant obeyed. She got up, scarcely took time to wipe her cunt that had been inundated with her own fluids, then went out of the room where the orgy was still going on.

Then she appeared behind the window next to Anne-Luce who seemed to be questioning her. Rose told the actress something

103

satisfying, no doubt, because she looked at me again and smiled. The two women talked for a while longer, while Anne-Luce continued to look at me with great interest, then her maid left her to come back to the room.

'Anne Luce likes you very much,' she said. 'The description that I gave her of you interested her and she wishes you to join her.'

'I am very flattered,' I replied.

Without hesitating, I left the room and went to the stairway that led to the door behind which the famous star was waiting for me.

She was wearing a short blue dress that was very tight-fitting about the waist and showed off her lovely figure. Her welcoming smile lit up her face and made her very likeable. She received me like a real hostess, as if she had known me for a long time.

'How are you?'

'Very well, thank you.'

She took my hand.

Later I learned that she had an American lover who had taught her these direct approaches. She led me to a room that was elegantly furnished like the others, but unoccupied.

'Do you like this?' she asked.

'Yes, very much,' I answered, a little intimidated.

'No one will disturb us here. We can get to

know each other,' she said, locking the door. Then, coming over to me, she drew me to her and kissed me.

'You're very beautiful. I love bodies like yours. Unfortunately, they are very rare. You have a certain grace that always overwhelms me. I am particularly sensitive to your kind of beauty as other people are sensitive to a look or a particular kind of intelligence.'

I was a little perplexed by this passionate, but unexpected declaration. Anne-Luce was capable of great enthusiasm. She was at the height of her richness and power and could permit herself to indulge in any caprice she wished, even the most unreasonable ones. She threw her arms around me, kissed me again, and then, moving away, murmured:

'Oh no, I don't want to bend you to my will or submit you to my desires. I'm dying to be your obedient partner, your submissive mistress, your slave. I would like you to order me and treat me like a weak woman. Tell me what you would like to do. I will be happy to obey.'

I was still overwhelmed, and nevertheless enchanted by Anne-Luce's proportions. She had to insist several times, until I dared to reverse the roles and act like her superior.

Finally I ordered: 'Undress!'

With the air of a victim, Anne took off her dress. I was sitting down and I told her:

'Walk slowly around the room so I can see you.'

The actress was wearing a short, white, transparent slip trimmed in lace. One of her breasts was sticking out. She continued walking around like a fashion model for five minutes. I loved it. She smiled when she was facing me, filling me with great desire. Then she turned around and walked away from me, swinging her ass in imitation of the positions destined to excite me. Her slip was tight and short, and the generous fruits that she was carting around were tightly compressed in the white sheath. Pressed against one another, the actress' tits looked like a huge bulge, parted in the center only by a median line. They looked like a pretty ass. The rounded nipples were pushing vigorously through the thin material.

Anne walked slowly, often leaning forward. I was so happy to be there, that I showed my satisfaction with little clucking noises and furtive little darts of my tongue over my lips. I kept my hands clenched in my lap. I was sitting on an ottoman and I followed the evolutions of my companion up and down with great attention, enjoying the furtive little looks I got at areas of her body that were still unknown to me, more than benefiting from the large horizons that she was revealing. I adored feeling my desire rise,

106

increase, and go on in different directions. Anne-Luce continued to walk and did not seem to tire. She never tired. What I desired, she gave immediately and skillfully. I loved her in her short slip, walking from one end of the room to the other, arching her chest, making her breasts stick out, or arching her back and showing off her ass. I liked her for doing all this to please me. When I thought: 'I will do this or that with an amorous partner,' I was happy to know in advance that it would be accepted.

Suddenly I realized that Anne was beginning to tire.

'Do you want to rest?' I asked.

She smiled and came over to me. I motioned to her to stay where she was.

'You must rest a moment. Get on your knees and turn your back. There! that's perfect. Stay that way and relax. Think of whatever you like.'

This permitted me to think of what I wanted myself.

Anne got on her knees and leaned on her arms, her face in her hands. From where I was sitting, I could smell her perfume. It was as sumptuous as the decor. Anne couldn't see her effect on my face, nor touch my clitoris which was darting excitedly like a dwarfish prick, furious at being so tiny and not being able to fuck.

What a wonderful spectacle! We see women from too close range. We never see them from far enough away to get a precise idea of what they are — not just their parts, but their whole erotic entity. Well-placed mirrors often permit us to contemplate ourselves making love, but there you are also involved and your vision is fleeting. Here in the room with Anne there were no mirrors, no movements. Just a silent, full panorama, immovable and yet mobile, candid, a stimulating fantasy of shape and color.

I wanted to admire her while she was moving again. I leaned over her and pushed my tongue into her ass. She moaned with pleasure but I wanted to torture her for a long time. Then I lifted my head and asked:

'Please, my love, take me from behind with a godemiche. I would love to have you fuck me in the ass.'

'Get into position for me,' she answered.

I obeyed immediately and waited while she opened a drawer and took out a leather cock. I felt her fingers gently part my buttocks and then her false prick being inserted with unbelievable force. She began fucking me vigorously. Her cock came and went inside my ass like a real member. I was in pain at the beginning but this was the best of all. It was splendid, powerful, and delicate at the same time. Soon I discharged.

Then I began to suck Anne's ass again and she discharged in her turn, crying out loudly like all women of delicate nature who experience everything intensely. We were still for a few minutes, savoring the passion we had just experienced. Then my hostess rang a bell and a pretty maid came in with a plate of refreshments and cakes.

Suddenly Anne remembered:

'Oh, I've forgotten my friends. I was in a room with some very amusing companions when I went out into the corridor and saw you through the window. I left my guests for you and now, if you like, we could rejoin them. I'm certain you would like them.'

I agreed. A few minutes later, as naked as I had entered the room, I left it and followed the pretty actress.

There were two men and two women in the room: Corinne, a splendid redhead with a large body; Odile, a tiny brunette with blue eyes that looked glazed; Robert, a young tall, thin, blond man with an aristocratic face; and Max, a dark, heavy-set man of about forty. All of the people in the room were bisexual. When I arrived, Max was buggering Robert who in turn was fucking Odile in the ass. Corinne was resting and watching them with a blissful smile.

Anne and I were greeted with exclamations of joy because we could bring some variety into their orgy. The actress, a true nympho-maniac, soon became excited by the spectacle of the trio and took her place on a footstool with her legs parted. There she began to masturbate.

Max asked me to put on one of the dildoes and screw him. I refused the pederast's offer, however. Of course, I wanted to do it, and the other women told me to, but I was still embarrassed in front of strangers. Max was furious and grumbled to Corinne and the actress:

'Isn't there some woman who will come and suck me? Please? I need to have someone suck my ass!'

Anne got up in a leap and went over to the pederast. She got between his thighs and began the task of licking him. Max groaned with pleasure.

'Oh, it's good! Your tongue is rough. I love that! Push it in further!'

Corinne was next to me when Odile called to her:

'Come here please! I need someone to suck my cunt. Hurry!'

The redhead didn't want to leave me alone, but she turned around and excused herself:

'Please allow me to leave you to go to my friend.'

I nodded.

She hurried over to Odile, who, lowering

herself between her pretty legs, stuck her tongue into her dilated cunt.

Odile whispered:

'Oh, that's good, Corinne. You always lick my cunt so well. Faster please. And deeper! Oh, it's so good!'

Now I was alone and terribly excited. Anne asked me to come over and screw her ass. I accepted immediately because I suddenly wanted to abandon myself like the others to the most bestial orgy. I went to Anne and inserted my false member. She screamed with pleasure. I fucked her with unbelievable strength. Now there were only moans and cries in the room. Robert was crying like an animal.

'Oh, it's marvelous! I'm coming! Oh!'

At that same instant, Max discharged in Robert's ass.

Odile was now uttering inhuman cries. She was begging Robert to continue fucking her, while Corinne licked her cunt.

Suddenly Odile whispered:

'I made it! It's over! Oh! I can't go on!' With that, she fell back.

Now there were only three who had not discharged: Anne, Corinne, and myself. While I continued to fuck Anne I saw Corinne get up and go over to the table that contained the collection of godemiches. She tested several before making her choice. Finally she picked the largest and thickest, tied it around her and, coming over to me, exclaimed:

'Please let me put my dildo into your ass. You'll see how good it is to be fucked.'

I didn't answer and Corinne pressed herself against me, caressing my thighs. Her leather instrument was dangling from her and exciting me considerably. I would have liked to ask her to put it into me immediately but even though I wanted it, I was afraid of the pain it would cause me.

I kept quiet as I continued to fuck Anne. As for Corinne, her caresses became more and more precise, her rod pressed harder and harder and harder against me and I trembled with desire. I began to fuck Anne more violently which made her moan more and more voluptuously.

Suddenly I realized that she was reaching the paroxysm of lasciviousness. The odor that her rear was giving off was strong and provoked a strange desire in me. Suddenly her eyes looked like they would pop out of their sockets and with saliva running out of her mouth she turned around and asked me quickly:

'Darling, I'm so excited that I have to come.'

'I'll let you, Anne,' Corinne said, 'but only on the condition that Svetlana permits me to screw her. Convince her and I'll give you permission!'

Anne answered without asking my opinion.
'Go on, screw her at once!'

Then I felt Corinne's godemiche become
heavier between my buttocks and her long,
fine fingers separated me. I felt the tip of the
enormous leather instrument pushing against
my opening which wasn't accustomed to a
tool of this size.

Finally a great pain overcame me and
spread out through my entire body. Corinne
had pushed her dildo into my rear. It was the
first time I had had such a gigantic rod in my
ass. At first I felt a sharp pain but that was
soon replaced by an exciting warmth. I was
a man whose cock was penetrating my
partner's ass at the same time that I, a
woman, was being penetrated by a male
member of extraordinary dimensions.

Now Corinne was fucking me harder and
harder. She pushed her tool in as far as she
could. I was panting as loudly as Anne and
our cries and moans seemed to excite Corinne
considerably because she turned around and
said:

'I also want to be possessed. I need a
man!'

'Come here, you, and take me.'

The man she had chosen looked at her
indifferently:

'No, I don't feel like it. I'm not hard
anymore. I just discharged.'

'Come here and let me have your cock. I'll suck it and make you want to fuck again!'

Robert walked over to us and Corinne immediately grabbed his prick. She began by biting the tip and then, seeing that he had puffed out a little, she swallowed the whole thing. But the fact that she was fucking me and sucking Robert wasn't enough for her.

'Odile, come here and take me in the ass! I'm terribly excited. I need it! Come here please.'

Odile lifted her head and then got up. She went over to the table of godemiches and tied one around her. Then she came over to us and separating her friend's buttocks, introduced her leather tool. Corinne screamed with pleasure. Then she began uttering the moans of a strangling animal.

Anne also began to cry:

'I want to feel a cock inside me! Come here please, Max, and fuck me!'

Max had gone limp, and turned around in horror! The actress went on begging someone to fuck her. She was trembling so hard that my godemiche popped out of her ass several times. Since no one answered her demands, she separated her thighs and put her own fingers inside her. Then she began to masturbate violently. Her cunt was so open that you could see right into it. There was a white liquid coming out. She rubbed herself harder and harder but couldn't seem to reach the final pleasure fast enough. Then she suddenly leaned over to a nearby table and grabbed the two biggest godemiches. She parted her enormously dilated cunt and stuck both leather pricks into herself.

Seeing her masturbating this way with two gigantic dildoes excited me very much and I increased my assaults on her ass.

Suddenly Anne fell back on the floor, crying:

'I'm coming! I'm coming!'

I discharged at the same time.

Several minutes later, Corinne, who was still being fucked by Odile's dildo and caressing Robert at the same time, also came in an ecstatic flood. The splendid redhead uttered a throaty cry and fell back, exhausted. But my friend, Odile, who had not ejaculated yet asked:

'Corinne, caress me. I haven't made it yet! I want to so bad . . .'

Hanging on to the woman with fire-red hair, she began to cover her face with tender kisses. Soon the two women were rolling on the floor, holding each other tightly and kissing frantically. You could see their tongues seeking more and more erotic sensations.

Suddenly Odile cried out:

'Look how big my cunt is, Corinne. Come on, fuck me!'

Corinne leaned over parted her friend's cunt, and began to poke her with fingers. They moaned together and Odile finally came. But the orgy wasn't over yet. After a brief intermission spent talking, listening to music, drinking, and eating, we began all over again.

It went on until dawn. I'll never forget it!

CHAPTER VIII
Felicia

At the time Felicia came into my life, I was particularly interested in women, so much so that I was going around dressed as a man.

One evening a friend of mine invited me to a party given by a rich industrialist. I saw several handsome men in his apartment, but what really caught my eye was a ravishing negress.

There were little plates of sandwiches on the tables and the liquor was flowing freely. Couples were already beginning to go off to corners. Most of the creatures of the weaker sex were already lying under their companions, their dresses lifted, giving themselves up to exciting activities.

I was sitting alone on the divan watching all the couples enjoy themselves. The costume I was wearing was a little too form-fitting for a real man. Suddenly while I was smoking peacefully, a young girl came over to me and asked brazenly:

'You are alone, sir. Wouldn't you like to make love to me?'

I smiled nervously, wondering if I ought to reveal my true nature. The girl was magnificently developed and was wearing a cream-colored satin sheath that made the dull lustre of her skin stand out. She smiled weakly and added:

'If you're not excited, don't worry. I can suck your cock and turn you on.'

And, with the spontaneity of an adolescent, she got down on her knees and unbuttoned my pants. Then she let out an 'oh' of surprise. She had just discovered my hairy cunt instead of the man's cock she had expected. She raised her eyes and I noted that instead of looking embarrassed or pulling away, she seemed to like it. To confirm my opinion, she lowered her head and stuck her tongue into my hole.

I trembled and opened my thighs instinctively. I helped her take my pants off and soon my lower half was naked. The young girl was sucking me in a marvelous way and I was already writhing under her skillful caresses. She caressed my ass with her other hand, the one that wasn't caressing my cunt. She was touching me in all the most sensitive places and I soon came, uttering little grunts of pleasure.

All the couples on the other divans were imitating us. Those who had just discharged got up and went over to other couples in order to become excited again. The unskillful ones were admiring their friends and then, having learned something, were trying to copy them. Others were hurrying off to the buffet to stuff themselves with food.

Then a splendid brunette, very tall, with a magnificent body sheathed in black lace entered the room and began walking slowly from one table to another, saying a few words to each person and generally showing off her beauty. Some of the men were trying to block her passage but she always refused with a smile. An English soldier tried to take her by force but she pulled away.

'No, don't touch me yet. I'm much too subtle for you to possess me with such grossness.'

Then a black athlete went over to her and, seizing her in his arms, covered her with passionate kisses. He pressed his lips to hers and soon had her trembling under his caresses.

The athlete, excited by the woman, wanted to fuck her, but she turned around offering her ass. The man hesitated an instant, then, leaning on his partner's shoulders, he penetrated her wildly. He fucked her for a few minutes and then came almost immediately, with a deep moan.

Although he had taken his pleasure, he did not leave his companion, who was still trembling. He couldn't seem to get enough of her. Then suddenly growing stiff again, he let his hand go down between her white thighs. He recoiled as if he had touched something scalding, and cried out violently:

'Bastard, you fooled me! you're not a woman, you're a man! This is horrible! I just fucked a fag! You disgust me!'

Wild with anger, he began to beat the 'brunette.' But the pervert seemed to be taking pleasure in being beaten by another male and he leaned back excited. The disgusted negro abandoned the homosexual and left the room.

Then the transvestite went over to one of the men and, removing the strapless bra that had fooled all of us, he said:

'You, come here. Let me caress you a little. I'd like to see you naked. You're so handsome! Undress.'

The man obeyed and stood naked before the fag.

'I like to take men. Come here, show me your ass. Oh, I love your body. First bring your cock up to my face so I can suck you a little.'

He began to suck his partner's tool which grew stiff immediately. Then, turning around, he stretched out on the floor and began fucking him in the ass. Soon they both discharged at the same time, and got up without even bothering to look at one another. They went over to the buffet, no doubt in order to eat something to regain their strength.

The whole scene had interested me very much and now I was caressing Felicia's breasts passionately. Meanwhile, the man who had disguised himself as a woman approached the young boy again and proposed to favor him with his services. The boy accepted and immediately stretched out on one of the couches with his ass up. His partner leaned over and I saw his tongue foraging inside his buttocks. The other boy was beginning to writhe with desire, and shouted:

'Fuck me, don't make me wait. I want you to take me like you took my friend before! Hurt me! Hurry! Your cock must be stiff enough. Do it now!'

But the first man replied:

'No, I don't want to yet! I'm not ready. Look, I want to, but my prick isn't hard enough!'

'If that's all it is,' answered his partner, 'I can suck you and make it stiff.'

'No, rub my ass a little. I think that's the only way I'll be able to regain the strength to fuck you.'

His partner began caressing his companion's buttocks, and soon we were all able to again admire his splendidly stiff cock. He turned his companion around, adjusted himself, and inserted his enormous prick.

'Oh, you're finally inside me! Push it in deeper. Oh, it's so good to be taken by a man like you!'

Excited by his young lover's words, the fucker began charging him harder and harder. When he pulled out he would wait an instant before repenetrating him with a rage that was doubled by the passion in his friend's words were engendering in him. The audience around them encouraged them with obscene shouts. Finally the first pervert began to beat his partner on the back calling him 'bastard,' 'trash,' and 'dirty fag.'

He accepted all the blows with great joy, writhing on the couch. Finally he began to moan:

'Oh, I'm coming, I'm coming! Oh, it's good!'

But his companion hadn't taken his pleasure yet and continued to fuck him. Soon he also began to discharge.

I turned to my pretty partner.

'What's your name?' I asked.

'Felicia.'

'That's a pretty name.' And what do you do in life?'

'I walk the streets.'

'Oh, good! Then you're in the same business I am!' I cried.

She laughed.

'Do you like to be beaten?' I asked her next.

'That depends upon who is doing it and how!' was the reply.

'I love flagellation,' I admitted. 'Would you like me to . . .'

'If you promise not to be too cruel and stop as soon as I ask.'

'I promise.'

Always prepared in advance to satisfy my vice, I carried a child's cat-o'nine-tails with me that I had bought at a bazaar. It no longer had all nine tails in question, but the leather of the lashes was hard. I moved it slowly over my companion's body, caressing her breasts, her stomach, her shoulders, and her face.

Felicia remained quiet, attentive, as if paralyzed by fear. I whispered to her:

'Don't you feel well? Perhaps you're still upset over the shock of a while ago? Do you want me to whip you harder?'

She did not answer so I leaned over her and began to beat her with precise little blows. Felicia pushed her abdomen out in a sudden contraction of pain, and began to writhe. To quiet her I applied a big blow across her thighs. Then I beat her torso, becoming excited by her voice and movements. The black girl who had contained her reflexes up to now and had scarcely been audible, suddenly began to scream. Delighted, my eyes enlarged with lust, a smile on my lips and saliva running down my chin, I beat her again. Now I was taking my time, trying to affect her, even waiting until she was apparently calmer, only to surprise her anew each time.

Wild with pain, Felicia tossed about with a series of sharp yelps that punctuated the dull shock of the lashes.

'There there, my beauty, look how you're changing colors,' I said without tiring in the least. 'Wait, here's a spot I seem to have missed!'

And I tormented her almost mechanically until her whole body was progressively turning pale and was being marked with long violet streaks.

'Enough . . . enough . . . please,' she begged. 'You're hurting me too much . . . Come, I'm yours, you know it. Make love to me, darling. Only stop, please, stop!'

She no longer knew what she was saying. She wanted to keep her composure and to control her reactions and at the same time not to excite me any more. She knew that I was getting gradually wilder and more distracted.

I no longer had the desire to possess her after having punished her a little; now there was the light of murder in my eyes, in the sickly feverishness of my movements. Felicia strained to get control of herself so she could fight back. If she could succeed in arousing me again I might stop beating her. Suddenly she pretended to faint. I stopped hitting her.

Felicia opened one eye and seeing me occupied between her thighs, she said:

'Now, do you want to beat me or fuck me?'

'Fuck you!'

I put on my godemiche and pushed it into her black pussy. She cried out. Her throaty sensual voice was in unison with my attacks. I withdrew a little and felt Felicia move with the pleasure I was giving her. This incited me to relieve myself of my needs. I pressed myself against her, put my hands under her and pushed my fingers in, pushing harder and harder in order to weld our two bodies together.

'Not too fast please, not so fast . . .' she murmured.

I held myself back in order to keep from finishing prematurely. That would have spoiled her pleasure which I wanted to be immense.

I pulled back, pushed in, pulled back again and watched myself in her eyes. For the moment I pushed aside the sadistic thought that was going through my mind.

'Now, faster,' she said. 'Faster, hurt me. Hurt me!'

She dug her fingers into my cunt and began to rub me with wild rage. While she labored over my body I was making her flesh sing. I could barely hear the jerky words she uttered. I came with a great orgasm that crept up on me. I felt it as a sudden, burning flow that ran through me and reverberated from the place of my union with Felicia up to my neck. I fell back, broken, my eyes dull, my hands wet, my lips parted.

Felicia became my mistress, and her body kept all the promises it had made that night. Beside that, she had a great imagination. We seemed to complete and compliment each other. On certain afternoons I would curl up in a chair and my brain would summon up past memories to create future fantasies. I was constantly searching for novelties.

Of course I would pout whenever she told me of her affairs. Then I would search for traces of unknown kisses that might have saturated the girl's body and I would caress the remains. She would moan and tremble, showing me her favorite places and enumerating her recent experiences.

The frequency of our lovemaking had united our respective natures and ultimately I thought I knew Felicia completely. I knew the lines of her mouth, her ears, the lobes and the fold where her hair began. Then her neck.

In my mind, I descended from there toward her chin, taking care to avoid her lips so I wouldn't be tempted to stop there for too long!

Finally I arrived at her breasts! I thought of myself feeling the contact of her skin, hearing her heartbeat, accentuating in unison with mine, with our reciprocal desire. I could see her nipples stiffening under her clothing, then her breasts themselves which became taut and hard when I licked them. From there, would go slowly down toward her navel, that trembling center. I loved the light down of her armpits so sweetly perfumed, the contours of her waist, her hairs filled with such strong odors! I could even hear the little moans she uttered, see the jolts her legs would make to prove that her whole body was a source of joy. And yet, in one night everything changed.

I had awakened before dawn and noticed that her place next to me in bed was empty. She had deserted our common bed. But where could she have gone? I didn't ask her. Instead I decided to follow her, knowing that her explanations might have been lies.

Several days later I was awakened by the door closing and I just had time to put on a coat over my nightgown and run after her. Soon I saw Felicia walking along the sidewalk in front of me. She went to a street of ill repute and walked into a very famous brothel. I hesitated an instant then decided to climb the steps and go inside.

I walked into a vast room. Felicia had just disappeared behind a door covered with a heavy red velvet curtain. I turned around and went over to a kind of reception desk and spoke to the person there.

'Excuse me for bothering you, but I would like to see the young woman who just went through that door.'

The woman smiled.

'Why, that's Felicia! She's one of our most sought-after girls, by the feminine as well as the masculine clientele. If you like, I can introduce you. At the moment she is taken, but if you will wait a while, I might try to arrange a meeting.'

'No, don't bother,' I replied. 'If I could just have a room from which I could watch the young woman . . .'

The procuress smiled at my desire.

'Oh, I see. Why, nothing is easier if you are prepared to pay a good price.'

'I understand that,' I answered immediately, already licking my lips at the thought of the spectacle that awaited me. The procuress led me into a very luxurious room in which one of the walls had a cleverly hidden slit through which I could see everything that was happening on the other side. I sat down in an armchair and posted myself behind the observation place. I didn't have to wait long.

A splendid man of about thirty was lying on a huge bed, peacefully smoking a cigarette. He had hardly taken more than five puffs when the door opened and Felicia appeared.

He got up and went to her. Felicia looked at him seductively and sat down on one of those beautiful chairs that the room contained. She crossed those legs whose perfect outline had always made me tremble with desire, and eyed the man provocatively:

'Well, what are you waiting for?'

The man moved closer to her and slowly began to unbutton her dress. She wasn't wearing a slip and a very pale lace bra made the deep shade of her skin stand out even more. Her panties, a minuscule triangle, were of the same color as the bra. Her legs were sheathed in very fine nylon stockings with black seams. Her strong breasts stuck out of the bra, making her more exciting.

My lover's partner seized one of her breasts and began to rub it with obvious delight. He slid his unoccupied hand into her panties and approached her slit. I imagined myself in the man's place, as I had been so often, foraging in my lover's pussy, and I grew insanely jealous. I knew from the look on Felicia's face that the man was caressing her clitoris. She moaned, almost cried out. I was hopelessly in love with my mistress and excited just from contemplating the couple's actions. I understood Felicia's supplications very easily.

'Take me, my love,' she cried. 'Oh, it's good! Come take me, please, take me . . .'

The man pressed her to him tightly and lowered the panties down her legs. I could see her cunt now with the curly hairs that I loved so much. Her partner wanted to fuck her from the front, but Felicia turned around and said:

'No, I prefer you to take me from the back.'

Her companion smiled.

'If you wish! You know I can't refuse you anything!'

His voice was that of an intelligent, cultivated man. He pressed himself against her and rubbed his enormously stiff cock against her posterior. But suddenly he said:

'Put one of your legs on the bed so I can penetrate you better. I like to fuck standing up.'

Felicia accepted immediately and the young man inserted his long member into her ass while she moaned:

'Oh, it's so good! How I love your cock! Oh, push it in further!'

She was gritting her teeth. I could see the outline of her clenched jaw as she pressed herself against her partner, and cried:

'You're marvelous! Your prick is fucking me so well! Oh, again, push it in again!'

The man, encouraged by these words, fucked her harder and harder. Suddenly Felicia demanded:

'Hit me, beat me. I won't be able to come if you don't do it. Go on, slap me!'

The man immediately executed the girl's orders and began to beat her. My mistress abandoned herself totally to the man. 'Fuck me harder, even harder. I'm going to come! Oh, I'm coming, I'm coming!'

She fell back and discharged at the same moment as her lover. They were silent for a few minutes, then the man got up and went to a room that must have been the bathroom. I could hear the sound of running water. He came out quickly, got dressed, and leaned over his mistress. He kissed her hand, silently and in a very dignified way, then left the room.

Several minutes later, a ravishing redhead entered and asked Felicia if she was ready for a second client. Felicia said she was and the girl brought in a young man of about twenty.

He was very tall and slender, with blond curly hair.

Felicia had put on a dressing gown and she held her hand out charmingly.

'Good evening,' she said.

'Good evening,' he returned. 'Allow me to

131

give you this in return for your services.' He gave Felicia an envelope which she took and placed on a little round table. Then she approached the young man and, wrapping her arms around his neck, took his lips in a long kiss. When she had finished and they had caught their breath, she announced:

'Tonight I feel like being fucked in the ass. Please be nice and do it that way.'

The young man smiled.

'I'd be delighted!'

'Then undress,' said Felicia who leaned toward him and began helping him take his clothes off.

Soon the young man was naked. He was thin but his body was exciting Felicia no doubt, because she rubbed herself provocatively.

'You're not hard, darling! Well, I'll take care of that!'

So saying, she pushed her cunt against the man's quivering cock, and slid her right hand over his balls. Her unbuttoned robe did not stay on for long and she was soon naked in her companion's arms.

'Well you certainly get stiff quickly!' she teased. 'Your rod is big enough to fuck me now.'

Then she turned around and presented her splendid ass. The excited man leaned forward and kissed it passionately.

'You're so beautiful,' he murmured constantly. 'You're really wonderful!'

Suddenly grabbing Felicia's shoulders, he penetrated her in a single blow. Felicia moaned at first then her cries turned into sighs of lust.

'Oh, it's good, my love. Bite me at the same time. I still want to feel the pain! Please push it in deeper. Bite me hard. I'll come more easily that way.'

The man obeyed but as soon as his teeth entered my lover's flesh, she discharged. The spectacle of this woman who had just known the supreme ecstasy excited him considerably and he came in his turn, letting his sperm flow into Felicia's ass.

In a few minutes the young man got up to leave. But Felicia, who was, no doubt, excited again, caught him and tried to kiss him again. The adolescent did not seem to be excited by it and left her almost brutally without saying a word.

My lover seemed disappointed and immediately rang for the redhead again. Felicia said:

'That man excited me and now I want to know new pleasures.'

'Very good, dear,' replied her companion. 'Maybe I can profit by it.'

'No, not yet,' answered Felicia. 'First bring the old man in and then we'll see.'

The redhead obeyed and opened the door for a small old man. He came into the room with his eyes bright with lust and immediately went over to Felicia. He kissed her neck and then broke his silence.

'Let's not waste any time!' It's been so long since you saw me!'

Without awaiting an answer, he began to undress himself. Soon he was totally naked, horrible, frightening, almost monstrous, his flaccid cock dangling between his fleshless thighs.

Felicia got on her knees and murmured:

'Don't be afraid. In a few minutes you'll be stiff. Even if you don't discharge, at least you'll know some pleasure when I put your cock in my mouth.'

She had seized the old man's member between her lips and was darting her tongue at it. She caressed his balls with her free hand. But the old man still wasn't hard. Suddenly he asked:

'If you will, my little beauty, please beat my ass and I'm certain that my rod will stand up again.' He stretched out on the bed and presented his rear to Felicia.

'Beat me, dear. Hit my ass! I like to feel it – it brings back my youth, the time when the most handsome men in Paris came to fuck me! Beat me harder, little whore!'

While touching the old man's testicles,

Felicia beat him with her other hand on the back, then on his ass, then back to his shoulders and down again. The old man was panting.

'Oh, it's good! Beat me even harder, please, my dear. I want to suffer even if I must die from it! Beat me!'

Felicia obeyed the old man's injunctions. Suddenly the little man began to stiffen and babble in an almost trembling voice:

'There it is, I'm hard, I'm hard, I can feel my prick standing up! Oh, it's good, you're marvelous!'

Felicia wanted to see her work and turned the old man around like a pancake. In reality, his stick was standing up proudly between his white thighs.

'Since you're hard, put it in me now,' she said.

But he answered:

'No, I don't want to. You know very well, I would risk death if I discharged.'

'Too bad,' replied Felicia.

Again she called the young redhead. The woman arrived immediately as if she had been posted at the door awaiting this call.

'Come here,' said Felicia. 'Look at this old bastard. He doesn't even want to fuck me!'

'That's a shame,' replied the young beauty. 'To refuse to caress a creature like you!'

She leaned over Felicia and began to kiss her, saying:

'With me you can do everything you desire.'

Soon the young redhead was running her hands over my beauty's body. Then she got on her knees and I saw her tongue penetrate my lover's pussy. Felicia was breathing like a little panting dog while her lover sucked her and excited her terribly. Then she murmured:

'Your sucking isn't enough. I need something more exciting.'

'Ah, that's true, I can't satisfy you . . .' murmured her disappointed companion.

Seeing her unhappiness, Felicia whispered:

'Don't worry, darling, we'll arrange it immediately. Go get your brother. I saw him a while ago.'

'Yes, you're right. I'll go at once,' replied the white girl.

She left the room and came back a few minutes later with a lad of about sixteen. He was very tall and awkward-looking.

'Oh, I love him!' cried Felicia.

She immediately went to him and began to kiss his cheeks almost maternally, all the while undressing him gradually.

The young boy was soon naked in front of the women and terribly embarrassed. He tried to leave but the two women held him back. Felicia got on her knees and, seizing his little prick in her mouth, began to suck him. The boy looked astonished. When she had managed to get an erection out of him, she turned to her friend and ordered:

'Now that I'm in full form, go get your two friends, those pimps. They have great cocks and will make me come. With you three, I'll be able to get excited. You fuck too poorly for me to be able to make it with you alone.'

The young redhead went to the door and returned in a few minutes with two tall men with the bodies of athletes. Felicia looked at them, went to them and rubbed her cunt against them. Then she said:

'Now it's the three of us. You will fuck me from the front while your friend buggers me.'

While speaking she had undone their pants, pulled out their cocks, and begun to caress them. Soon, both pricks were stiff. When Felicia judged that they had reached sufficient dimensions, she offered herself.

'Now, I'm terribly excited. I want both of you. Take me together and make me suffer! And you other three watch us,' she added, addressing the old man, the child, and the redhead.

The two pimps approached Felicia as if they were executing carefully planned, precise ballet movements. The youngest of the men put his cock into her cunt while the other penetrated her ass. Being fucked by both men, she found herself pushed from one side to the other, but she always succeeding in following the rhythm and in moving at the opportune movement so that both cocks would hit her at her most sensitive places. She moaned and writhed with pleasure, but still did not come and she cried out:

'You, my pretty redhead, let me suck your cunt. You must be dying of desire.'

The beautiful girl did not have to be asked twice and immediately went over to my lover. She began to lick her and bite her and the redhead uttered cries of pain and pleasure. Then Felicia wanted to caress the old man's cock as well as the boy's with her free hand. She called to the two males and as soon as they were in reach she began moving her skillful fingers over their pricks.

I never got to see the end of this party because at that moment the door opened and the madam came over to me.

'Do you like what you've seen?'

'Yes,' I answered, panting, my eyes glazed with lust.

'It excites you?'

'Enormously,' I answered.

'Could I satisfy your desires,' she proposed. 'Would you like me to?'

'Gladly.'

I was ready to take anything that fell into my hands at that moment. I spent the rest of the night making love to the procuress.

Two days later, my beautiful Felicia found death in a car accident with one of her lovers.

CHAPTER IX
The Dancers

After Felicia, my life became very dull – just little fucks to earn my living as a prostitute, until the day I met Mr Varennes, the director of the famous Parisian cabaret, *The Green Parrot*. He had accosted me in the street and made a pass at me and afterward he had offered to let me visit him one evening at his establishment.

'We could have a real orgy,' he had added. 'Come see me next Sunday when the ballet mistress, who is a real procuress, will be introducing her new pupils to me.'

I accepted and the following Sunday at eight p.m. I was sitting before the stage at the famous restaurant.

But the most beautiful spectacles for real connoisseurs of music hall entertainment are not always on the stage. How many of those enthusiastic spectators and those elegant women who applaud behind the champagne buckets would gladly pay anything to go behind the wings? But that's the forbidden world; its temple is closed to outsiders.

The evening was coming to a close at *The Green Parrot*. Perhaps I should say the night, because it was very, very late. I had seen so many exquisite and marvelous things, felt rich sensations, admired sumptuous, unveiled bodies. It would take at least twenty-four hours to digest everything that my eyes had taken in and my ears had heard. After resting a day, I might remember the details. Some particular scene might reappear in a sort of isolation. I might see the exquisite smiling faces of the girls or hear the ventriloquist's voice. I might try to retrace the dances or recall a jazz theme. But for the moment, it was over.

The great master of the house, Mr Varennes, justly proud of his spectacle, wiped his forehead. He knew quite well that he had nothing to fear, that everything was carefully regulated by skillful technicians. He also knew that there were people everywhere who saw to the order and discipline. But, the more sumptuous and grandiose the spectacle became, the more he sweated.

Finally everything was over again and the owner went into the wings.

'Very good, children. You were wonderful!'

Artists are always happy when someone appreciates their efforts and tells them so. To them, each vigorously applauded act is a battle they have won. Sometimes it is only accomplished with great difficulty.

I went with Mr Varennes. In the wings there was enough sex appeal to spare. I brushed up against naked shoulders provocative legs, and even naked sexes. You only have to put out a hand to touch the most beautiful legs in the world – those that make artists dream. But naturally no one ever puts out their hand. Those who might do it without danger don't care, because they see the same thing every night and were blasé because it is so much a part of their occupation. Others would probably be thrown out! But it was enough for me to look to the left or right to be delighted.

Laura Noel was in her dressing room. She was the star, and the directress of the corps de ballet. She had her hat on and her long skirt, but you could still see her adorable thighs sheathed in black silk. Laura didn't know she was being watched. She was busy with some mysterious task, opening a valise that needed repairing.

Mr Varennes cleared his throat. The star raised her eyelids and lowered her skirt at the same time. Too bad! She had shown us much more during the performance, but that wasn't the same thing. Now we were in her private world.

The most beautiful girls in the world were employed there as models, and backstage in the loges they were delicious. It was the time of relaxation and also for showers. Proudly they let us see their figures up close, and with good reason. They could read the admiration in our eyes.

I don't know who once wrote that there weren't any more pretty breasts. That sad and disillusioned mind would do well to go to *The Green Parrot*. He would rediscover his taste for life. A model we caught by surprise in one of the showers did not try to hide her chest with its stiff, full nipples, or her cunt with its exciting fur. The freshness of the water was reviving her, and her skin was sparkling under the spray. She was a goddess emerging from the sea. She said:

'You are very indiscreet!'

But why should she have been angry? Why hide that which put her in the category of creatures that are admired because they have received the marvelous and rare gift of perfect beauty? There were others in the room with perfect skins. They all had the same calm, the same certitude that physical beauty brings. But how far from the coldness of statues! Everything that we saw was warm and alive like life itself.

Then suddenly the quarter hour of relaxation was over. The naked beauties went

to dress and mingle with the crowd. There
they would be swallowed up by the masses.
They would no longer be goddesses, but just
'belongings.'

Mr Varennes introduced me to Laura Noel
as his new 'secretary.' But the directress must
not have been fooled and no doubt guessed
what my duties would be. She was very
pleasant and held out her hand in a friendly
way. We were to go to her house where the
whole troupe was waiting for us, along with
several invited guests and the new girls she
wished to employ in her ballet.

When we got to the party, there were four
beauties, completely undressed and as fresh
as they were different, awaiting us in a line.
There was a redhead, a brunette, a blonde,
and a girl with gorgeous auburn hair.

When Mr Varennes, Laura Noel, and I
entered the beautiful apartment, the
conversation stopped magically. Our hostess
turned to her employer who had taken a seat
in an armchair in front of the naked beauties
and said:

'Please, sir, come here and tell me if these
girls are worthy of joining your corps de
ballet.'

Mr Varennes got up and answered:

'I would like to try one of these novices, but
unfortunately I'm not aroused yet.'

'Oh, that's nothing,' replied the directress.

And, getting up, she signaled one of her dancers.

'Let me introduce Clara. She will show you what she can do.'

The young girl approached him and knelt at his feet. Then she began to unbutton his pants. She took out the director's cock, held it in her palm and began to caress it delicately while running her other hand over his balls. Soon the director's pole was visibly stiff.

'Now, my child, suck my prick. That's an order!'

The young dancer seized Mr Varennes' stick and began to suck the tip. Then, seeing the organ take on such huge proportions, she put the whole thing in her mouth. Soon the man began to writhe on the chair, obviously very excited. He got up, panting, and said to the young applicant:

'You're perfect, my child! You know how to suck magnificently! To reward you for your good services I'm going to fuck you.'

With these words, he took the little dancer and pushed her down on the floor. Once she was stretched out, he lay down on her and pushed his head into the girl's breasts. She manifested her pleasure by little lusty cries. Mr Varennes swallowed the young woman's nipples and bit them passionately. Then his hands descended toward the dancer's pussy where he encountered her white lace panties.

He dug his fingers into the delicate garment and began to caress her with great precision, while she cried out her encouragement.

'Oh, sir, you're so good at that. I love feeling your fingers inside my cunt! Oh, your caresses are exciting me. It's so good!'

The director, excited by the dancer's encouragements, grabbed his enormous cock and adjusted it at the extremity of his future employee's love-lips. Then he took her by the shoulders and pushed his enlarged staff into her hole in a single thrust. The ballerina uttered little yelping cries and writhed while her patron charged her violently. To excite him even more, she answered his blows with her strong buttocks. Mr Varennes' balls were striking her body and augmenting her excitement.

Oh, that's good,' she cried. 'Your prick is enormous. I love it! This is the way I love to be fucked! Oh, your cock is so hard!'

The director's face was becoming more and more strained. He seemed almost at the point of ejaculation. His rod would come completely out of the young woman and then enter her again in a single thrust, disappearing through her black hairs.

She continued to writhe and moan:

'Your stick is getting bigger, it's good! I'm going to come! Your prick is getting bigger! Oh, oh, it's marvelous!'

The director dug his nails into the girl's shoulders and assailed her even harder, whispering:

'Whore, you love being fucked. I'll hire you just to be able to screw you again. You'll suck me every day! Those will be your principal duties! Oh, you bitch, how I love your cunt!'

Then he suddenly fell back, screaming:

'I'm coming! Oh, I'm coming!'

Instead of leaving his cock in the dancer's box, he took it out and aimed it at the girl's face. She opened her mouth and swallowed her employer's sperm as it spurted out. The whole scene excited all of us.

Several minutes later, the director got up and addressing himself to Laura, said:

'That little whore is wonderful! Of course, I'll hire her!'

Then he turned to the young woman who had remained on the floor with her legs apart.

'But you haven't discharged! I'll take care of that!'

But our directress intervened and, with much delicacy, suggested:

'Naturally, Mr Varennes, I'm not opposed to that, but I would like our friend to occupy herself a little with your charming secretary who has honored us with her presence. That way she can show us her lesbian talents as well.'

Several minutes later I got up and began to

undress. I had on only a light dress that buttoned in back and it didn't take long to remove it. I left my panties on. The young postulant had gotten up and came over to me to caress my thighs. She gently introduced her fingers into my cunt. She was very skillful and the pressure of her fingers on my clitoris made me shiver with pleasure. From time to time she would pull on my hairs with the other hand, which excited me terribly. Then she began to suck me.

During this time, our employer had approached us and was sticking a superb godemiche into the young dancer's ass.

While holding her ass out to Mr Varennes, the young applicant began to suck my cunt. Her knowing tongue penetrated me and made me wet with desire. At each of Mr Varennes' blows her teeth would move against me. I moaned with pleasure and had a terrible desire to come. When we were all panting and Mr Varennes was hard again, our hostess came over to us and murmured to my partner:

'Tell me, Clara, would you like to fuck Mr Varennes' secretary?'

'Why, gladly, Madame,' she replied.

Getting up, she left me for a few minutes to go get a dildo. She tied it to herself and came back to me. Then she took me by the waist and, with several skillful blows, inserted her leather tool. I shouted with pain but I was terribly excited and the penetration agreed with my aroused senses. Mr Varennes profited by this new position and possessed Clara's ass at the same time. Then Laura Noel ordered one of her decorators, who was watching the scene, to fuck Clara's cunt.

The young man stretched out and Clara sat down on his prick so he could penetrate her. As she attacked me, she received the charges from her new partner. But Laura Noel still seemed to want to put the postulant's capabilities to the test and she called to one of her technicians:

'Come here and let pretty Clara suck your cock! Then we'll really be able to see what she can do!'

The young man went over to Clara who seized his prick and began to suck him furiously. That made five of us giving each other the most refined pleasure imaginable. I was at the height of my excitement. The moment was coming when I would have to discharge. Laura Noel then asked a new man to intervene so that Clara could use her unoccupied hands on him. The young girl obeyed and took his soft penis in her hands and rubbed him very hard, pulling on his balls until he finally grew stiff. Our hostess was delighted.

'Oh, she's wonderful! Isn't she extraordinary Mr Varennes?'

I admired her and yet was jealous that she was capable of doing so many things at the same time. I also wanted to show what I could do. I shouted:

'Someone bring me a godemiche because I also know how to use one!'

Instantly, as if she had been waiting for this to happen, a splendid blonde creature with a gold complexion and beautiful breasts and legs came over to me with a dildo in her hand.

'Tie it around my waist,' I ordered.

She obeyed. Leaning over me to tie the instrument around me, the girl parted her legs and allowed me to see inside her cunt. This spectacle excited me and I cried:

'Oh, you're beautiful! Come here and give me your ass!'

The girl came to me and offered me her bottom. Her buttocks were large but not displeasing. I grabbed her and inserted my false prick into her. She cried out. I pushed it in harder and harder and I thought I was going to come immediately because the pleasure I was getting was so intense.

But my perversity increased and I needed something else now. I shouted:

'Someone come here quickly. I want to suck!'

One of the technicians came over immediately.

He was a tall blond with a splendid body

and wide shoulders. His cock was stiff so I took it in my mouth and began to bite the tip. Then I swallowed the whole thing and his prick expanded to enormous proportions. I had rarely seen such a big one, except in pornographic photos. I sucked him frantically. The man was panting and his cries mingled with those of my other companions. I was too excited to come. I no longer knew where I was but I suddenly knew that if I had a man's cock in my cunt I would finally be able to orgasm.

'Someone come fuck me!' I demanded wildly.

I was to be satisfied by a small man with curly hair. He was short but his cock was more than respectable in size. He fucked divinely, but I wasn't satisfied yet. My hands were still unoccupied.

When I asked for a man, a makeup artist hurried over. I didn't like him because he was a fag, but I really didn't care. I wanted to reach the end of myself, to spend myself, to exhaust myself completely. We were all crying but over all the vociferations I heard my own voice shouting:

'I'm coming, I'm coming, I'm coming!'

What happened the rest of that night is now only a blurred memory of repeated ecstatic cries, fuckings and orgasms.

CHAPTER X
The Beauties and the Beasts

I had lived and loved a lot. And yet, one of the most exciting orgies was not to come until a year later. One of my lovers, a little old man who was generous and undemanding, had bought me a little villa that overlooked the sea. From then on, it became my second home, where I spent a good portion of the year.

In the beginning I didn't pay any attention to my neighborhood, but one day I learned that one of my tall garden walls separated me from the girls' school of that region.

I couldn't prevent myself from following the games and pleasures of the beautiful adolescents of sixteen to eighteen who engaged in their recreations so close to my home. From my room I could watch them and contemplate the prettiest among them through my binoculars. I took my time studying their legs, their waists, their varied bosoms – full or tiny, opulent or nubile, the faces that were innocent or not, shiny or dull, topped by long or short hair. Before me envolved a whole free harem!

I was content with the spectacle of these marvels, never hoping to get any more out of it, when a blessed event permitted me to penetrate further into the girls' privacy. One day while studying the layout of the school I noticed that the upper class dormitory looked out over a seldom explored and dense part of my huge garden. Desirous to know the nocturnal habits of the schoolgirls I went over to the corner of my property and stood behind the windows that had been thrown wide open because of the stifling heat. Instead of silence which, I had feared, I soon heard, as I had hoped, words and laughter. I climbed up on a rock and peeked inside.

At first I couldn't distinguish anything, but soon I observed the adolescents lying in their beds with the covers off because of the heat. I saw that several among them were not only naked, but were stretched out in couples in the most shameless amorous positions. So the schoolgirls, like other young girls locked up in those pail-like schools, had no other distractions than love. The beautiful creatures were embracing and possessing one another.

My eyes stopped on each couple and detailed their activities. A blonde with hair almost as short as a boy's, sensual lips, a sculptured body and a tiny waist, was fucking another beautiful creature through the use of a godemiche. Then my eyes were attracted by another couple; a girl of about twenty with copper hair and tiny breasts and a little negress with a rounded body were sucking each other.

I soon made out a third couple whose activity stopped me immediately because in this lascivious place each detail, as in a gigantic fresco, was a world in itself, a universe to be explored. A tiny Chinese girl with almond eyes was chirping in a frail voice as she offered her buttocks to her companion, a tall blonde girl who was licking her ass with indescribable greed. What an extraordinary contrast there was between the passionate European and the Asiatic girl who, while enjoying genuine pleasure, seemed at the same time to be smiling at their own situations.

But I couldn't linger over them, when other parties in the vast room were engaged in infinitely more interesting orgies.

In a corner of the room, a splendid brunette was being fucked by a girl with auburn hair while she rubbed another girl who was in turn caressing the first girl. The three adolescents were uttering lascivious moans that resounded in the night and even reached my ears.

'Oh, I love your breasts! I love to caress them.'

'Oh, it's good . . . Let me touch your pussy again!'

All these erotic words seem so ridiculous when I write them down but they were wildly exciting when I heard them from the mouths of those ravishing creatures.

In still another corner, as if sheltered from other eyes and too occupied with their own pleasure to be interested in their neighbors, a quartet drew my attention. A rather small brunette was being fucked by a girl, who, in turn was being buggered by a tall, slender girl, so thin that you could see her bones. The latter was being licked by various people. The four musicians of the quartet were not uttering any distinct words. All I could hear were moans and mumblings which were highly suggestive. The group was acting like a team of rugby players united in a championship match. The girls appeared preoccupied with a competitive performance more than with pleasure. But then, perhaps erotic love resembles such sport because of its climactic goal.

In another part of the room I discovered a strange trio. Three students were in a circle, looking at one another while masturbating themselves with their fingers and with dildoes.

Finally one of the spectators left the circle.

'I'm bored,' she said. 'We need other partners and I'm going to get them!'

So saying, she grabbed a raincoat from the closet and threw it over her short nightgown. Then she left the other girl without waiting for a response and put her hand on the door.

I heard myself cry out in spite of myself:

'If you need new partners, perhaps you'll use me!'

Their first reaction was total silence. Then there were exclamations of surprise.

'Who's there? Who are you? We've been betrayed!'

Having acted hastily, pushed on by desire more than by reason, I no longer recognized myself in the dialogue that followed. It was another person who was speaking in my place to explain herself, to explain me.

'I'm only your neighbor, the owner of the villa next door. I've been observing and admiring you for some time and very unhappy not to be able to participate in your charming affairs.'

My spontaneous, well-couched phrases produced the most wonderful effect. I sensed it from the approving murmurs that greeted it. Therefore, I felt that if I continued my presentation, coloring it with pleasing phrases destined to delight my juvenile public, I would achieve the desired effect. It worked, and the girls asked me to climb through the window and join them.

In a few minutes I was no longer an intruder. I was a guest who honored them with my presence and whom they greeted with signs of the deepest respect. I jumped through the window with the help of several of the girls. One of them who appeared a little older than the others, and who had an authoritative look about her as if she directed the little group of pupils, asked me to undress.

'We all want to see you naked to be more familiar with you.'

They made a circle around me and kept their eyes glued to me while I took my clothes off. I had a simple, nylon dress on and it didn't take long to remove it. Soon I was naked before them and it was with a joy full of pride that I heard their appreciations.

'Oh, she's beautiful! Look how long her legs are! And her breasts, they're splendid – not too tiny or too big. Her waist makes me want to put my arms around her!'

Then the young woman who had asked me to undress came over and touched my tits gently. She pressed her lips to mine and we lost ourselves for a few moments in the ecstasy of our embrace. She pulled away and, seizing a godemiche that was on one of the beds, she tied it around her waist. Instinctively, knowing in advance that I was to benefit by it, I stretched out on the ground.

She lay down gently on top of me and I felt the contact of her leather member on my vaginal lips. I trembled with delight and tightened my embrace. Soon I felt her tool insinuating itself inside my cunt. I moaned. The prick was enormous and it hurt to be fucked with such vigor. I was literally swooning in the girl's arms, as she sucked my tits while fucking me. I was panting and murmuring constantly:

'Oh, it's good. Suck my tits some more. Oh, I want it to hurt again. Make me suffer, please. Oh, it's marvelous! You're beautiful, my dear. Screw me harder, it's so good!'

Then I thought I could also give some pleasure to one of the other students.

'One of you come here, I want to suck a cunt!'

The splendid negro girl whom I had admired from my observation post approached me and rubbed her pussy against my mouth.

'Here, take my cunt in your mouth and lick it. I want to come that way,' she cried.

I immediately seized her cunt and began to lick her. The young girl writhed passionately. My tongue penetrated as far as I could and I rubbed her clitoris with my hand.

What followed next was a total confusion of the senses. I was fucked, sucked, and buggered, while I rendered the same services to other partners. But I won't linger over the description of all the joys I tasted that night with all those young creatures. I can only say that it was the most memorable night of my erotic life.

CHAPTER XI
Conclusion

My rich, full life is not yet over, but these reminiscences draw too close to the present for me to continue writing them down. I have described with great pleasure, the joy that my adventurous experiences have brought me, and offer them to the reader with the same generous wish for delight in which I experienced them. But certain parts of my life must remain secret.

I have lived here in the same villa for many years now. The girls' school next to me, where I tasted such happiness at one time was closed, but not before those young, beautiful creatures and I experienced countless hours of ecstasy. Some of the students came to live with me from time to time, and we shared a multitude of pleasures together. I also took young male guests, students at nearby schools, or simply adventurers, and we all explored every conceivable avenue of delight and happiness. One of these young men became my lover, a very handsome painter from Greece, as developed in mind as in body, a paragon of pleasure and beauty. Our world consisted of music, art, literature, nature, and of course, indescribable ecstasies of the flesh.

But as I continue to think of my past, I am aware of the present slipping away, and with it, the delights that still await me. To have written so much is enough, I think. To have experienced even more is better. I live on with the thought that there is still something new, and thrive on the hope that I will discover it, too.

THE SPANK
'EM PAPERS

PROLOGUE

LETTER FROM SIR CLIFFORD NORTON
TO HIS FRIEND MISS CLARA BIRCHEM . . .

My dear Clara:

An incident in my boyish life tonight passes
before me in all the tinting of a panoramic
view; and as my thoughts run back over the
checkered pathway of forty years, which has
sprinkled my hair with grey, filled my life
with thorns and orange blossoms, to a month
that has left its imprint on my whole life, I
wish that I possessed the power to reproduce
the picture in all its colours, and do justice
to the work which, at your request, I
undertake tonight. I regret that the favour
you ask is one which compels me to write of
myself; and in the perusal of this, I trust your
eye will rest on the unpleasant character I
am, as little as possible.

I was born beneath a warm sun and
pleasant skies; where the air was freighted

with the blended odour of the magnolia and jessamine that heightened the senses; where everything had its bud and blossom almost at its birth; where the dreamy languor of the voluptuary seemed inherent in all; where even in those who here in the North would be termed children, the sexual spark only waited for contact to flame up in its power; where girls were mothers at thirteen and grandmas at thirty.

My introduction to the pleasures and mysteries that have ever been associated with the couch of Love was not entrusted to a novice; no timid, simpering girl, taking her first steps toward the realisation of the anticipation of forbidden pleasures, but to a woman – a woman of thirty, who being an apt pupil under the skilful manipulations and teachings of a husband for a term of years, had herself become a preceptress in all those delicate points that surround an amour with such delights and rosy tints.

How plainly do I see her tonight! How much keener is my appreciation of the wonderful piece of anatomy, that time only still deeper imprints upon my memory; the standard by which from that time all female perfections have been gauged. Ah! she is before me again, and this time unveiled. Look at her! Is she not beautiful? Note the poise of her head, from which her glinted golden hair falls in such a wealth. See those amber eyes; those wonderfully chiselled lips, so red and moist; her fair cheeks tinted by their reflection.

See those shoulders – how perfectly and exquisitely moulded – rounded with the same finish as her beautiful, swelling globes, so daintily pinked and tipped. What belly, back and hips ever had the graceful curves of thine? And you! Rounded arms, white swelling thighs and full dimpled knees (in your warm, fond pressures of years ago I feel you again tonight) was the mould broken with your completion? Gone? Yes! Only in memory now.

My initiatrix snatched me from my little heaven with its delightful anticipations, and chaperoned me through the hot-house of passion, where every beautiful flower was filled with a subtle poison which racked the nerves, sapped the life and deadened the brain; and on that sweet, sighing summer day in my sixteenth year, when Cupid threw apart the silken drapery, revealing beauties of which I had not even dreamed, to books I said farewell, and ambition was dead. That was a day of fate.

In a dense shade, where the sun could not penetrate, we sat down on a log; and after she had taken off my hat and run her dainty white hands through my hair, she placed my head in her lap, and, pulling me close to her panting bosom, she placed her pretty lips on mine and held them there, with her eyes shut, until sometimes I stifled and almost lost my breath; then she would take her lips away while her eyes sparkled, and her cheeks reddened clear to her hair.

There was something about it all that I liked, for I would ask her to do it again; and she, exclaiming: 'Bless my little man,' would press me to her again, and kiss me until my lips and face were all wet from her lips. Each attack and each pressure seemed to create for me some new and delightful sensation I had not known before, and then, where my little pantaloons buttoned in front, I had a pain and a great hard lump that hurt me, and in my innocence I told her about.

'Let me see,' she said kindly; and one of her hands, that had so many pretty rings on her fingers stole, down and unbuttoned my pants; and then, what I had never seen more than two inches long, and soft as a baby's flesh, was standing out full five inches and terribly swollen. I was awfully frightened at the sight and the pain, but she took my young prick in her hand, kissed it four or five times and bit it gently, telling me 'it was no matter,' and I seemed to get better right away.

But I was perfectly passive in the hands of my fair seducer, and I suffered my pantaloons to be taken down, and myself to be thrown backwards on the grass. Her snowy hand eagerly flew up and down the dainty shaft of my cock, keeping the glowing head uncovered, and all the thread of the froenum well stretched. She stooped, and her tongue caressed the tip of my penis, while her other hand was making that magic tickling (called by the French, the spider's legs) on my balls, and up and down the urethra.

Suddenly my thighs stiffened out. I trembled violently and felt a strange sickening sensation. I believed that I was about to faint, as the white spunk, flashing out from my bursting knob and bedewing her cheeks and tongue with liquid pearl, fell in a tiny splash on my belly, whilst her swimming eyes were fixed on my spending prick, as it shot the jet forth.

Then she carelessly unfastened her chemise, and I saw what I had never seen before in that way – two beautiful bosoms at once. How pretty they looked, so white and so round. She rubbed them, panting and heaving, over my face and lips, and then whispered to me to 'bite them,' and as my lips fastened over the little hard tips, her breath almost burned my face, and I felt a new joy and realised that I was swelling again.

Then I felt one of her warm hands steal down and take my pego, while with the other she took my hand, rubbed it up and down on the big part of her soft legs, and then to the softest, prettiest thing I had ever felt in my young life, where she left it. Oh, what a plaything I had found, so soft, curly and juicy; and as my hand found a delicate opening, she jumped as though I had hurt her. Then I felt her open her legs wide apart, after which she whispered to me to get in there and lie on top of her, which I did.

As she pulled my little shirt up, I felt my bare belly fitting close to hers, and that her chemise was clear up to her arms. Oh! How she hugged and kissed me, and how nice her plump bare arms felt to my face and neck. I thought that she would break me in two. Whispering to me to do just as she told me, she reached down and took the little fellow that was killing me with pain, and placed it where I had my finger when I thought I had hurt her. 'Now you make it go in,' she whispered, and she raised her body with my weight on her, and when she settled back my prick *was* in.

She gave a great sigh, as I had heard people do who were in trouble. Then she squeezed me and bit me, and seemed to be trying to rock me in a new kind of cradle; and taking me by the hips, she would push me off and pull me back, never letting that little fellow get out of the nest, where she had placed him;

and while I felt a tingling sensation in my
fingers and toes, and up and down my back,
she would roll her head from side to side,
saying, 'Oh, oh, oh!'

My initiatrix suddenly locked her legs over
my back; then, bending her back, she panted
and held me so for a second, trying to reach
my lips, but I was too short. Then I lost my
senses and everything got green, and I felt
that I was bleeding in and all over that pretty
little plaything on which I had been lying for
ten minutes. Her arms and legs unloosened,
and I rolled off from her, shaking like a leaf;
but she kissed me, and whispered that I
would feel better in a few minutes, and I did.

Then she took me in her arms, telling me
that I *must never tell*; and asking me if it
wasn't awful nice, she kissed me again a few
times, made me kiss her, and with my head
on her pretty bosom, we fell in the most
intoxicating rapture. 'Wasn't it awful nice?'
Well, I should say it was; the little heaven I
had created had all been knocked by the one
she had created for me. I smile when I think
of my innocence – smile when I reflect what
a public benefactor I was at that tender age.

Imagine – friend Clara – how exciting it
is for a woman of thirty, well-formed and
knowing all things, how exciting it is, I say,
for such a one to clasp to her full-formed and
matured bosom, the slender frame of some

sweet youth; to press the thick golden forest of her curls, and full lips of her cunt, against the hairless shaft and balls of a lovely boy; to watch his first delight, to see him stiffen himself out and grind his pearly teeth in the ecstasy of a first spend, while she herself is lost in lustful delight at feeling her companion's hand wet through with the flowing spunk that follows his motions to and fro in her full-developed quim, drenching the thick curls through. It is this pleasure which made my beautiful seducer teach me this exquisite bliss.

Yes, that was a day of fate. In the afternoon, we strolled out into the woods. She was silent for a while, then turning to me she said: 'My little man, for you are a man, what we did is what those do who get married. My husband is sick, and for months I have been almost dying for the pleasure your body has given me so tenderly,' and drawing me to her, she kissed me rapidly. I felt very proud of myself after what she said, and immediately asked her if I might do it again; with a smile, she kissed me and said she 'would see about it.'

'I had a strange desire to see more, and I said: 'Mrs B—, you have such pretty legs, would you let me see them higher up?' She said: 'Why, certainly my little man, I will do anything for you,' and reaching down, she gathered her dress, skirts and ruffles, and held them clear up over her face. Gods! What a picture; the tight-fitting stockings, the blue garters above her knees, and the white, bare thighs. Then the skirts went down again, but the picture was left in my mind.

She who had so delicately taken my virginity knew the power her beautiful legs had brought upon me, and on the way back she revealed them at every opportunity; and when I asked her if I might put my hand on the little beauty spot, she said: 'Yes, but be quick,' and I was; but I did, and she liked it as well as I; and the reaching down, and putting my hand up, under her rattling skirts, to the mossy charm, created the same intense thrill that characterised the same attempt in my later years.

Again I peeped under her little shirt, and saw the white bare thighs that had held me so tightly. How beautiful and fascinating she was as she stooped to unlace her shoes, and drawing the stockings from her bewitching legs, as she stood up again. 'I like you,' I said to her in a low tone, and she replied: 'You little rascal, have you been all this time watching me?' I inclined my head, and whispered that I thought she was so nice and pretty. 'Bless your heart,' she ejaculated, 'do you think so?' I answered: 'Yes,' and asked if she wouldn't please take *all* off.

Looking at me a second, she shrugged her lovely shoulders, and the chemise slipped down to her feet; then I saw her all at once from her full neck to her toes – saw what I had longed to see – that little beauty with golden hair which had almost killed me with joy. 'Now are you satisfied?' she asked, and she bent over me, while her bosoms rested on my face; and as I put my hands on them as though to keep them, she put on her chemise – then took it off again – and was less than a minute in getting by my side.

My initiatrix was a magnificent woman; her bosoms were of immense size, her eyes beamed with lust and expectation, her thighs and bottom were well shaped, and the thick golden fleece of her quim reached nearly till her navel. She threw herself backwards on the grass, and suddenly opened her legs wide, driving two of her fingers deep into her large and thick-lipped coral slit; then lifting up and bending one leg, she forced one finger (having wetted it in her cunt) right up the corrugated brown hole of her bottom, in which it was sheathed.

Then she moved her fingers backwards and forwards in and out of both apertures. Soon she lost all control of herself and, grinding her teeth, she quivered with lust from head to foot; she moved faster and faster, and soon the most obscene words came from her lips:

'Oh God! Oh fuck! Oh fuck!' she cried, and then with a moan of delight, she arched her body and fell back spending, with eyes, large, dark and bright, fixed on the foliage above, 'Oh God!' she exclaimed, as she took out her fingers, and the spunk flowed in torrents down her thighs.

'Oh God! What bliss!' I knew now what she wanted; what I wanted; the ice had been broken. I was an apt pupil, and the secret fire of my youth had burst forth in all its fury. I bit her arms, her belly, her legs; bit and sucked her rosy nipples; kissed her from head to foot; tickled her little beauty with golden curls; got on to and off from her; put my head between her hot thighs, which pressed it until I thought it would split; sported from knees to lips in a wild delirium of newfound ecstasy, her breath burning my cheeks as I rested for a moment with my head on her beating bubbies.

Then, holding me tightly, my fair enticer put a sudden stop to my gambols, and sliding her hand down to her little friend, who had attained his majority – and was no slouch, I assure you – she put me on my back, and bending over me she nibbled him gently with her red, damp lips; and then, falling on her back, she lifted me, as though with iron force, above her.

Opening her quivering thighs, my lascivious

preceptress let me down gently, saying: 'All ready,' and taking in her hand the pet who was eager for his duty, she gently parted the golden hairs, and having fitted him, locked her arms around my body; then she kissed me, and, raising her buttocks from the grass, pressed gently up; my bare belly fitting close to hers, I pressed down, and she fell back with a smile and glowing cheeks.

The motion she had produced before in her way, when she had taken my *pucelage*, I now felt that I could perform it without assistance, and as I did so she tried to kiss me, and whispered: 'That's right,' her voice fluttering so that I thought she was choking. I had found the secret of her pleasure, and hers was mine; and as I alternately tickled her, briskly, then gently, I remember a suppressed, fluttering moan, which I now know was the acme of bliss. But I grew tired and fell where I lay; and yet linked together the bliss went on in a delicious throbbing, that cannot be told.

Soon my ruttish partner gasped: 'More! more!' and I, loving her so strongly that I would do anything for her, began again the gentle movement. She whispered to me, but I was getting deaf and blind with erotic rapture; and then I whispered to her that it was coming. She straightened her snowy legs, drew them together, threw her belly up against mine, loosened her arms, quivered from head to foot, gasped: 'Now then!' and as a thick mist gathered in my eyes, I felt the hot stream go from me to her, and all was over.

'Oh, you sweet boy,' said my handsome debaucher, as she pulled me up to her lips, kissing me and biting my neck, 'you don't know how happy you have made me – how you have satisfied my restless, burning fever.' As happy as a lark, I ran my hand all over her beauties here and there, petted the little flaxen-haired darling, crawled up to her bubbies and nibbled them awhile, and then, with her kiss upon my lips, I fell asleep, while she was smoothing my hair, and the sun, shining through the grove, was lighting her beautiful, velvety skin with a rosy tint.

After dinner, we went down to the boat for a ride. She talked to me while I rowed and kept my eyes on hers, and observing that once in a while my eyes glanced towards her little feet, she seemed to know by intuition what was in my thoughts, and up went all that hid what I longed to see. The sight sent the blood to my white face, and, as she put down her skirts, she looked at me and, smiling, said: 'My little sweetheart, if you will row to some nice, quiet little spot, where no one goes, and we can be alone, you can lie between the legs you think so pretty and like

177

so much.' I pulled up to the point, and we came to a nice little grass plot, on which we sat down, after she had spread out a light shawl.

'Oh! Ain't this nice?' she said to me, 'what a nice time we will have alone in the shade'; and putting her arm around me she fell back on the shawl, taking me with her. We were both on our backs, looking up among the green leaves. Soon she drew me closer to her, and asked me what I wanted, and as I placed one of my hands on the bosom of her dress, she began to unhook it at the neck one by one, until all were undone, and I saw them peeping out over her chemise, so white and round; then she unclasped her corset.

By this time, I was on my knees, and unbuttoning her chemise, I turned the corners back and took the pretty things, all undressed, in my hands. Then I bent over them and kissed them, bit them gently, then sucked them, and it seemed to me then, that I would have given my life to have one of them all in my mouth. I was feeling good all over as she pulled me down to her, and kissed me in such a new way that she seemed to cover my whole mouth with her lips and suck it all in between them.

I felt her hot tongue in my mouth and almost down my throat, while her breath came hot and her bubbies rose and fell. I turned and saw her skirts above her knees, and as with one hand I reached down to pull them up higher, so as to feast my eyes, I felt her hand working into my pants and tickling the little eggs that I thought would burst with pain. I had just got my hand on the little bird's-nest, that was such an infatuation to me, when she said: 'Jump up quick and take off your pants.'

As I arose to do her bidding, and unbuttoned my pants from my jacket, what a delightful view I had of her many charms; and those bare thighs! How intensely inviting do I remember them. My pants off, I walked to her and stood over her, my soldier standing hard and proud. She put out one of her hands and took hold of it, and then raised herself until her lips could touch it. Oh! How she squeezed and bit it, all the time muttering some little words of affection.

Then, springing from me, my fair initiatrix leant over a log, and I sat on my knees, between her legs widely straddled apart. Thus, just over my face, I had a view of a magnificent bottom, with its corrugated brown hole, surrounded by little ringlets of hair, red shot with gold, and pressed out between her thighs, the thick velvety lips of her enormously developed cunt. I, conveniently placed, pressed my face against the red flesh of her luscious quim, and darted in my tongue.

179

Her outrageously lustful passions soon showed themselves; convulsive tremors shook her frame; her crimson cunt opened and shut on my tongue. She supplemented my efforts by frigging herself on the ruby-button in front. Soon the crisis approached. I heard her murmuring: 'Prick – cunt – fuck – spunk,' till at last, with a spasmodic contraction of the cheeks of her bottom, a flood of spunk, creamy and thick, shot out, like a man's, over my face and bosom, and ran down her own thighs. I kept my head down between her white legs, and kissed little goldy until she rolled and moaned, and said she could stand it no longer. 'Do it now! do it now!' she said, and as she threw her thighs apart, I crawled between them, and rested my weight on her belly. Then I felt her warm fingers arranging things; and she had placed her pet as she wanted him, I felt him among the parted curls that were all wet, gliding so smoothly until the whole shaft was all in, and our bodies were fitted close together.

'Oh! what delight!' she seemed to be doing the same thing with her mossy lips that she had with the others, when she kissed me a few moments before; and I felt that she would draw me to her very heart, body and all, as she lay there, murmuring: 'Oh, you sweet boy! Now, you do it to me nice,' as I drew back gently my rampant prick, and then plunged it back quickly.

I felt her body writhing under me with some new motion of her buttocks, that I had not felt before, which was highly electrifying to us both; but how wet and smooth she was there. Soon she began to draw her legs up, and then straighten them out again, her hands squeezing her bubbies, while, with her eyes shut, she rolled her head from side to side, a gentle moan escaping her half-open lips.

'Now! Now! Quick! Quick!' she said, as she opened her eyes and started suddenly. I felt that I was dying with delight, but I immediately began knocking more vigorously at her little gateway, and as she locked her legs over my back, holding them so tight that I could not move, I felt a tingling, twitching sensation of delight, and in a second her velvet-lined lips were sipping the hot stream of my youthful passion. Her arms fell lifeless at her sides; her legs dropped from my back, and the smile on her beautiful face spoke more than words.

Ah! how that woman, on that day of fate, had crept into my life. I was hers, body and soul; she was my sunshine, my life; no thought that was not of her, no act but that tending to gain her smiles. I could look in her face and eyes for hours and never weary of it. Little did I know then what the heart was; what it could suffer; what it could stand; and yet how short was the time until mine was put to the test. The days came and went, but there was no abating in my desire to see her charms; to know the delightful intoxications that I found in her arms.

My mistress did not always humour me in my desires, however, knowing that for her pleasure I must have time to recruit to be equal to her passion, but she was always kind and gentle, and outside of the *act*, never denying me a wish in the looking at or feeling what I chose. Yes, the mould was broken after those hips and legs so well shaped. How often, while standing, has she allowed me to stoop down and get under her skirts, and with my arms around her hips, let me bury my face high up between her swelling thighs, until I almost suffocated.

Then she would lie and lift her legs in the air, bending her knees; my hand was passed between her legs, so that my finger touched her ruby-button enshrined in golden floss; my other hand was passed under her thighs and my finger embedded in the gap which, like a scarlet slash, opened between the golden curls. Swift motions followed, and soon the crisis came. I saw the pearly drops of love oozing out, as her frame trembled with lust.

It was over; she lay with her head thrown back, her lovely thighs apart, and from between the swollen lips of her vermilion slit, streamed the sweet drops of creamy spending.

I loved this hot-blooded voluptuous woman who gave herself up to me entirely, and humoured every sexual caprice, and knew every whim and fancy. Her kisses were of fire; her lithe limbs twined round me; her lips wandered over every part of my body; her fingers, with their magic touches on my cock, my balls, my bottom, drove me mad with lust; her cunt, warm, wet, thick-haired, and spending, drew the very life blood from my heart; and as I often died away between her soft thighs, her skilful touches never fail to rouse me again to action.

What woman could equal my lecherous seducer? Who could mount on the top and, engulfing my prick in her quim, exercise that power of internally clipping grasping and squeezing my rod by inward pressure, in the convulsive throbs of supreme lust, called the 'Nippers'; not forgetting to vibrate her pretty, rounded bottom, and so draw forth the fountain into her womb? Or who, lying upon me, could rub her sweet, fair-haired slit on my mouth, and by hands and lips revive my drooping shaft, till it shot its treasures over her agile tongue? In fact, on my back, with her lustful cunt on my face, her tongue and lips, responsive to mine, could draw forth that liquid bliss, that the *other* lips have failed to elicit.

In the midst of the luxurious course we were running, she could softly babble such bawdy words as might excite me more; and as she murmured: 'Fuck! Fuck! Cunt! Spunk! Frig me! Fuck me!' urged me to the sweet end. Lastly, when my pego longed for 'fresh fields and pastures new,' she could even present her bottom, with its soft curves, to me, and, parting its cheeks with her jewelled fingers, show me the rosy and crinkled aperture of Sodom, in which tight sheath I could shoot my sperm, into her inmost recesses.

Owing to her large and swelling breasts, my fair one could even practise the 'bosom-fucking'. She lay on her back, and as I placed my stiff and glowing prick between her bubbing bubbies, she pressed them together on each side, so as to embed completely my penis in the warm and snowy crease. Now I moved to and fro, and up and down, the purple head appearing and disappearing before her enraptured eyes, till the sweet crisis, when the jet of spunk shot out, and the slippery stream deluged her breasts. Her feelings were then so roused, that a few insertions of my finger or ticklings of my tongue in her burning vagina brought down her magic flow of bliss as well.

In short, as a woman to please, my lascivious mistress was most complaisant, and *stuck at nothing*. She even allowed me with delight to penetrate her quim, at those periodic times when 'the red flag was flying' and when all men know women want it twice as much, and love the man who lets nothing stand in his way, and is wise enough to know his darling is better than ever then.

One day, my fair debaucher wished to go to the city and return in the evening. On her promise to take good care of me, I was allowed to accompany her. On arriving we went to an hotel, and were placed in a lovely room. After closing the lower shutters, she began taking off her clothes, while my eyes were wide with wonder; one thing and then another were taken off, until finally she stood with nothing on but her stockings and chemise. She seemed to hesitate a second, and then taking those off, she threw herself on the bed with her hands over her head.

How sweet she was, and as I stood looking at her, she said: 'Come, my little man, ain't you going to take yours off, and come and lie with me?' I was going to be in heaven again, and I had mine off in half the time she had taken, and was as naked as she, when I stepped up and stood beside her. At last, I had a chance to fuck my darling in a cosy hotel, as a smart dandy does. But I failed, at first, to perform my duty on that particular occasion.

Yes, I got into bed with her, and I failed utterly, partly, no doubt, from over-anxiety, partly nervousness. Dr Johnson said that 'a woman ought to take off her modesty with her petticoat.' My lewd mistress found that such was the case. She pretended to take no notice of it, but by sly touches, many caresses, and exhibition of her lovely naked body in many attitudes, endeavoured to make the best of what was but a momentary feeling, caused by a too eager desire to please her, and a nervous anxiety for the last sweet favours she was ready to grant completely.

Taking her playmate in her hand, so soft and white, she tickled him awhile and saw him grow, and after nibbling me a little on my belly, she threw her arms around me and tossed me over on the bed, and, straightening me out full length, she drew me close to her hot skin and covered me with kisses. As soon as she loosened her embrace, I had my mouth on one of the nipples of her snowy breast (and as I remember now, that act struck every electrical wire in my body – it does yet).

My hand was over the little 'poulter' nestling in the soft of her thighs, and as my finger found its way in slowly, she rather liked the two sensations. Her cheeks growing redder each moment, she grasped the fellow who, at his full size, was throbbing at her side, then, jumping up quickly, she took the pillows, and throwing them together on the bed, told me how to lie on them. When she had me bent over them to her idea, that, which she was longing to feel wedged in her mossy lips, was standing up hard and proud.

Then the method was for the fair one to lie on her side, on the bed, as I lay half facing her, and half on my back. Then lifting up her upper leg and laying my face on the lower thigh, I could see the lovely golden-haired cleft, and press in it my lips and tongue, and as her upper thigh remained raised, I could, whilst gamahuching her, see the lovely curls and ringlets that ran back and fringed her arsehole. This left my hand at liberty to frig fiercely her bursting clitoris, which excited her madly, as it does every woman. As she was tickling my balls with her soft hand, her crisis soon arrived, and her warm thigh fell on my face. I saw her arsehole throb and her cunt spend enormously, as it shot out in jets, and completely drenched my arm. It was the glorious spending, swimming quim of the full-blown and lascivious woman of free passions.

As soon as she was recovered, she got over me in the right position. I felt her place my fleshly weapon between the hot velvety lips, and after a gentle motion on her part, it was all in, where she seemed so delighted to have it. 'There, now! ain't that nice!' she asked, with a look of mingled joy and pride, and then she began to slide up and down on it (in a peculiar way that I have not known since), her bosoms jumping with every move that seemed to send fire through my veins to my brain.

I could feel that she was making me awful wet where we were linked, but the sensation was hot and delightful; and as she kept at work, I saw her grasp her bosoms, as though she would crush them. Her motion became more rapid, her lips swelled, she shut her eyes and threw back her head. She flung out her arms and drew them back again, and as she trembled all over, my delight reached its height; and as my love messenger took wings and flew, she fell forward on me with all her weight, almost crushing my bones.

She lay panting and gasping for a moment, and as she jumped to the floor, I saw that he who had given her so much comfort, also my belly, bore delicate crimson stains. She saw it, and blushing deeply, said it was no matter, and sponging me off, I put on my shirt, and lay with my face to the wall, as she had asked me to do. Soon she came with her chemise on, and taking me in her arms, we went to sleep, my face resting on her white bosom.

After awaking and imprinting a lustful kiss on the crest of my youthful cock, my salacious mistress, exciting herself with her middle finger for a short time, threw herself over me, so that she knelt astride of my face. Then lowering herself a little, and throwing herself forward, she presented to my enraptured view her magnificent buttocks, and her corrugated pink bottom-hole surrounded by tiny curls; and beneath the splendid coral gash of her lovely cunt, with its inner lips spread open, gaping with expectant lust, and the glorious golden bush of hair covering her mount Venus and running up, as I before described, to her navel.

My ruttish initiatrix then pressed her luscious quim upon my eager mouth, and my tongue revelled in the moist and lovely scented gap, and travelled round the prominent button, taking it into my lips and sucking the crimson knob of her clitoris, which was of immense size, from so many scenes of love and lust. Nor was she idle; as she took the whole of the head of my prick into her mouth. There, we laid belly to belly, devouring, kissing, licking each other's sexual treasures; each with a busy finger tickling the arsehole I with one hand moulding her breasts from below, she my balls.

We indulged in the most intoxicating lasciviousness, but this could not last long. Our bodies writhed, her rampant cunt seemed to expand and take in half my face; my bursting penis seemed all within her mouth. With a smothered cry we both spent, and the white sperm bubbled out of the corners of her lips in pulsating throbs, while her thick and slimy spendings deluged my face. We both swallowed all up, and fell apart, gasping with fierce delight. But, like Messalina, my lewd mistress was *'lassata sed non satiata'*, wearied but still not satisfied. After a last kissing, we arose and dressed, and at nine were at the cottage.

The last rapture that I ever knew lying between her voluptuous swelling thighs was on that day she took me with her to the city; and that night my young, boyish heart felt its first aches and trouble. Two days after, she kissed me sweetly at the gate, saying that she would never forget me (it has been mutual). She let me get in her snowy arms, she allowed me freedom with her bosom, but with any attempt to put my hand under her chemise, she took it away, saying: 'No; no more.' My fevered brain sketched and re-sketched the beautiful life figures, which she had unveiled to my eager eyes; and the spark she had discovered and fanned was burning me alive.

After long weeks, I was victorious and, when strong enough, returned to school. But ah! In those days, my prurient seducer injected into my veins the sweet poison which has remained for years; and I sacrificed health and ambition. Trusting that in the perusal of this, you will be – Dear Clara – rewarded with all the pleasurable emotions that you anticipated, – that I have written nothing to burst the front buttons from the trousers of your young gentlemen*, or bring the dear girls to the use of a long-necked *cologne* bottle to quench the flame in their electric generators – my task is finished.

---

* *Miss Clara Birchem was the handsome and voluptuous governess of a school, at the time she is here introduced.*

CHAPTER I
Harry

A fine-looking, fresh-coloured youth named Harry Staunton, the son of a London merchant, sent down to the village of Allsport for the benefit of his health, was passing down a lane skirting the town, when his eye was caught by a young and handsome girl whose fully developed legs were beginning to make the short skirts she wore dangerously exciting to the gentlemen who visited at the house of her mamma, who were obliged to curb their desires and satisfy the excitement of their pricks by closely pressing her to them when they could get her into their arms for a romp.

It must be admitted that the warmth of the young lady's temperament urged her to afford them this opportunity as frequently as possible although she could not account for the pleasure it caused both her and them. They would tickle her round the hips and under the arms and pinch her bottom and occasionally press her lovely bubbies.

Miss Wynne was in the act of fastening her garter when Harry turning a corner of the lane came suddenly upon her. As this was not the first occasion of their meeting, Julia neatly put down her clothes and waited for his approach. He came up and took her by the hand and she with a flushed face expressed her pleasure to meet him again.

The night before they had been playing forfeits with some companions and as the game went on, it so happened that she was kissed by Harry who without knowing why slipped his tongue in her mouth and kept it there till his young prick throbbed against her so violently that she felt it against her belly through her clothing.

All the evening afterwards they sought every occasion to be together. On one occasion several fell down on each other and Harry and Julia being underneath, there was sufficient time for him to get his hand under her clothes, insinuate it within her drawers and then to feel her soft warm thigh and afterwards her cunt which was just covered with a soft down.

Julia did nothing that night but dream of feeling Harry's tongue sucking her own as he was kissing her and reproducing the same sensation, she had felt when his finger penetrated just inside the lips of her cunt.

Before morning she had renewed the feeling by the agency of her own finger and only ceased to frig herself, when an emission came to her relief. It was no wonder therefore that she was glad to meet her lover.

Harry placed his arm round her waist and pressing her towards him kissed her and slipped his tongue into her mouth. She met it with her own and as they curled amorously around each other, he not only made her feel his standing prick pressing against her as on the previous evening, but taking her willing hand made her squeeze it.

'Oh, Harry, what is that?' the pretty little creature murmured pressing her finger tightly around it of her own accord.

'Put your hand, dear, inside my trousers and feel,' he answered pushing against her as if to make it penetrate her even through her clothes, while she pressed against him with equal force.

Unbuttoning his trousers, she thrust her dainty little hand inside and felt his prick which was so hot as almost to burn her hand.

'Feel it, dear, while I feel you,' he cried again and, stooping until he got his hand under her clothes, he passed it upwards between her thighs, and seized her cunt preparatory to putting his finger in it.

Prompted by her sensations, the young lady had that morning left off her drawers and Harry, on finding the glowing and palpitating flesh all naked to his touch, took his arm from her waist and raising her petticoats up around her, groped her hips and bottom with one hand while he frigged her gently with the other.

She, lifting up his shirt, had taken his cock in her hand and, taught by nature alone, while chafing it began to place it near his fingers. They were just on the verge of actually fucking when to their chagrin they were disturbed.

Coming towards them from the other end of the lane was Miss Birchem, the handsome and voluptuous governess of a school for young gentlemen. She had espied the amorous occupation of Harry and Julia and had seen the excited youth take up the young lady's clothes, so that her white bottom had thus been exposed to view.

The governess had also seen that which caused still more emotion in her own quim – the prick of the handsome boy fondled by the hand of the girl. The sight had maddened her and for a moment she had been compelled to lean against a tree, which prevented her from being seen by them.

While her legs trembled under her, Miss Birchem had raised her own clothes above her cunt, parting the hairy lips of which she had thrust her finger in it up to the first joint and commenced to frig with rapidity her sensitive clitoris.

This she continued to do, her breasts heaving and her whole body oscillating under the influence of the sensations she was experiencing, until she saw Harry and Julia in that close contact that had the appearance of actual fucking.

This brought her feelings to such a height that, with a gasp and a quickened movement of her agile waist the governess spent, to such an extent that she almost shrieked as her spunk issued from her.

At this moment Harry had just placed his prick inside Julia's quim who was lying prostrate and the girl would have lost her maidenhead had not the young man restrained himself.

Just as he had partially penetrated her quivering body and she was kissing him passionately, the crisis came upon him and he shot forth his spendings on her clitoris.

This caused Julia to embrace him still more closely, curling her leg around him so as to get him further into her in her desire for a continuance of the pleasure she had hardly tasted.

Miss Birchem however came upon them and thus interrupted their amorous sports.

This lewd governess had a mad passion for flagellation, preferring first to have her own buttocks well birched by a gentleman while he was frigging her with his finger to assist her in spending.

She next liked to flog the buttocks of a gentleman, watching its effect on his prick, especially if he was at the same time fucking a girl, increasing his excitement from time to time and tickling and momentarily sucking his testicles till she at last caused him to spend with a shower of rapture, during which crisis she would flog him unmercifully.

Seeing the charming bum of Julia when Harry raised her clothes, filled her with a burning desire to whip her while Harry's prick was buried in her own cunt, as copious spending had not quelled the lust with which she burned.

Julia drew down her clothes and Harry tried to hide his prick as the governess confronted them. But she seized them both at once, young Harry by his prick causing its head to erect itself as much as ever at the contact of her hand, and Julia by her half-covered thigh, saying:

'Oh you wicked children, what are you about together! What has he been doing to you, Miss, with this naked cock of his? Do you know it is very wrong of you to let the boys put their things into your cunt until it is covered with hair like mine? See here.'

And, giving a furtive squeeze to Julia's quim to ascertain if it had been spent into, the governess glancing lewdly at the young man, pulled up her own clothes, displaying to the fascinated eyes of Harry, limbs of surpassing beauty, covered with attractive silk-stockings.

Miss Birchem had thighs smooth and white as ivory and a belly of ravishing sweetness below which was a tuft of dark hair which was moist from her recent emission, while in the midst of it could be seen the pink lips of a full but closely shut cunt.

'There, Miss,' she said, enjoying the admiration with which Harry viewed her beautiful quim, 'you must wait till you have hair like this on it, before you can enjoy the insertion of a prick as I do.'

'It does give me pleasure now,' said Julia fixing her eye upon the swollen prick of her lover, rather than upon the handsome nude limbs of the lascivious governess.

'But it ought not to, and I shall give you a good whipping for your wickedness,' said the lewd and sensual woman, her whole form glowing with excitement as she gloated on the lovely bottom of Julia, which she had wholly uncovered.

Miss Birchem then left her victims and gathered a huge handful of birch which was growing all around them, and Julia blushed as she saw her tying it together with some ribbons that she took from her pocket, the bottom of the prurient maid tingling with the mere anticipation of what she was going to receive, a sensation not altogether unpleasant but novel.

Now armed with this verdant rod, the salacious governess took Julia by the hand, saying: 'How I must whip you to correct your naughty feelings, but as you have excited me by allowing me to see you take this young gentleman's prick in your cunny, I must insist on his putting it into mine.'

'When I was your age,' continued the libidinous woman, 'a gentleman put his cock into me, but he hurt me so dreadfully by fucking me that I have never been able to allow any one else to do so, nor could I marry for this reason, therefore I am compelled to take young men to fuck me and Master Harry here must do it now.'

'Come to the bank,' resumed the ruttish governess, 'and sit down so that you can take me on your lap and put it up from under me while I am taking Julia across my knees, to give her a warning that she must not be fucked again until she is more of a woman. There is no one near or to disturb us while we are doing it.'

The lecherous woman now made Harry sit

down upon the grassy bank. His prick was erect and hard and throbbed violently with desire to be in the beautiful fornicatress, as she raised her clothes behind her, displaying once more her glorious legs and thighs, with the most superb pair of large buttocks that was possible for a lady to expose.

The lustful Miss Birchem then seated herself, with her legs well divided according to the bawdy manner, upon the lad who, in his eagerness to thrust his hot burning prick into her dark cunt, seized her around the waist, creating a jealous feeling in the mind of Julia to see how readily he was prepared to fuck another cunt than her own.

The concupiscent governess once more seized the young man's prick and sitting down upon it, guided the moist head – not into her cunt as he expected – but up her bottomhole which Harry found quite elastic enough to receive his tool.

Excited as he was, the youth began to fuck her there violently, as though he was buried in her quim, while the indecent woman taking up Julia's dress all around her, thus unchastely exposed the cunt of the lovely girl as well as her bottom.

The voluptuous governess now made the virgin lie across her thighs, keeping her between them and holding her victim in this position by passing her right leg over, shuddering with lust as the naked flesh came in contact with her own.

The shameless woman then gently separated the buttocks of the tamed girl and examined with looks of fire the lovely little pink hole which looked like a pouting rosebud. In the clutches of such a Messalina, the unresisting maid quivered with the anticipation of what she was going to undergo.

The debauched woman actually laid her finger flat between the cheeks and gently pierced the pouting rosebud, an action which caused Julia to press violently against the thighs of the governess and contract the muscles of her bottom.

The governess then seized the birch and commenced to flog the pretty girl with sufficient severity to make her indulge in such contortions as to afford most delicious sensations to the operator.

When Harry's prick was buried in her bottomhole to the very balls, Miss Birchem grew nearly frantic with delight and continued lashing Julia's naked bottom with a vigour that increased with every subsequent thrust that Harry made in her bottom.

CHAPTER II
Miss Birchem

Miss Birchem, when she said that no gentleman could fuck her, was romancing. She had originally been mistress of a nobleman, Sir Clifford, who having passed a life of voluptuousness in the society of women who had seconded him in all his whims and strange desires, had at last required more stimulus to his passions than they themselves could afford.

At first his *outré* desire was to enjoy her posteriors by birching them. This she submitted to at first to please him but afterwards to please herself, because under her correct and modest outward appearance burned a violent fire.

She soon conceived such a mad passion that she implored her lover to administer the birch to her burning posterior, an indulgence he never denied her, no salacious wantonness being sufficiently voluptuous for her.

The baronet's mistress soon became in possession of outrageously lustful passions for flagellation, and the sensations were so delicious that she suffered physically and mentally, when in the impossibility of satisfying her sensual desires.

At length her cunt did not seem tight enough round his prick when he fucked her. Then on one occasion, when he had been severely flogging her as she knelt on the bed projecting the cheeks of her naked bottom, he proposed to fuck her in her inviting anus.

The rod had generated such a heat in all her private parts that she imagined that it would give her pleasure to receive him there and she therefore consented. With his prick inflated to its utmost, he leant over the naked creature whose burning face and palpitating breasts were half-buried in the downy bed.

Bringing the point of this prick opposite the orifice he wished to enter, he gave a lunge and succeeded in getting a portion of it into her body. At first it gave her such an exquisite feeling that she encouraged him in his attempt to get farther in.

But as his cock stretched her wider open and appeared to enter with much difficulty, she tried to shrink from him. He was however too much excited to stop, and her extreme tightness and the heat of her posteriors goaded him on.

Sir Clifford had been holding his mistress by both her shoulders, but now he passed one hand under her breasts to feel and move those luscious orbs. The other hand he carried down below her belly and seized her burning cunt.

Opening its velvet lips, the baronet sought and found her clitoris, which he rubbed gently about with his fingers and thus worked upon her venery to such an extent that she was capable of bearing anything.

Thus simultaneously frigging her mistress and driving his prick into her anus, she at length received the whole of his enormous tool fully within her, having thus a double pleasure conferred on her.

Miss Birchem's body now was bathed in blissful heat, their motions kept pace with each other, the room resounded with her sighs and exclamations of enjoyment and the luscious sound so exciting to the ears of the voluptuary. At length her movements grew so rapid as to announce the near approach of the crisis.

Her lover felt he could no longer refrain from spending. Both gave way to their feelings and the baronet ejected a flow of spunk into her body, while his hand was wetted with her emission which oozed out from her convulsed and struggling quim.

From this time Sir Clifford more frequently fucked her mistress in this way than in any other, until the novelty having passed off to a certain extent, he had an idea that he should like to see her fucked by another, while he stood by and watched the effect on her and the performer who was buried in her quim.

The nobleman had as usual stripped her perfectly naked and for a change had taken her across his lap, in which position she threw her handsome legs about under the infliction of the birch. Each time the lash fell upon the crimson cheeks, Miss Birchem cried out:

'Oh heavens! My bottom, my backside! Oh flog it, whip it, birch it, flagellate me harder, harder, lash me darling more severely. I can bear it as hard as you can lay it on your mistress. Oh you must put your darling prick into me after this!'

Wildly excited by her cries, he said: 'By heavens! I will, I must!' Throwing the rod aside and taking her in his arms, he laid her on the bed. She turned upon her back, her thighs wide open and her cunt instinct with life, showing such muscular throbbing action of the lips that it inflamed him to the utmost.

The baronet leaped upon the bed and lay on her upheaving form, belly to belly, then with mouth to mouth and tongue clinging to tongue, his marvellous cock entered that longing cunt and she threw her legs around his loins and her arms about his neck. Too full of bliss to speak for a time, she frequently withdrew her tongue from his mouth and asked:

'How do you like to fuck me like this once more?'

'Intensely, you enchanting girl,' he replied.

'What would I not do to give you pleasure, anything, everything – for your prick is so divine – but you are spending into me too quickly,' said his mistress, as she felt the burning spunk leap from him into her.

'I cannot help it! Oh God, you are so beautiful and your cunt does throb so.'

'But I want to be fucked till I spend,' urged the lewd woman, willing to indulge in the most intoxicating lasciviousness.

'Will you let William fuck you then while I am witness to the pleasure you will give him?' said her lover.

'Anything that will afford me delight,' replied his ruttish mistress.

Sir Clifford got up and dressed himself, while she still lay in the position she was in while he was enjoying her, her lovely limbs stretched out, playing with the rosy nipples of her lovely breast which were standing up stiff and hard.

When he had put on his coat, he stopped first to kiss her cherry mouth, then for a moment to suck her enchanting breasts and then her lovely cunt which she elevated to meet his caress. Then, throwing the sheet over her, he left the room.

The baronet shortly returned, accompanied by a fine handsome youth in page livery. He had called him into the library when he departed on his mission, and asked him how he got on with the maid and whether any of them had yet taken his maidenhead.

The boy of sixteen, blushing like a *pucelle*, said with the utmost confusion that he had never done anything to them or they to him.

'How William,' said his master, 'how would you like to be with a naked woman? Would you enjoy her quim, if she would allow you to fuck her?'

William did not know what to reply, but his master perceiving that his prick was commencing to bulge out the front of his trousers, decided for him and conducted him to his mistress who had been frigging her cunt the whole time he had been away, in order to keep her excitement from cooling.

Fastening the door, Sir Clifford led the lad up to the bed, took his hand and carrying it under the sheet, slowly passed it over her legs and thighs and left it on her spending quim, an effect her frigging had just produced.

Seeing that his blood was heated by desire, his master slowly turned up the sheet as high as his mistress's breasts, leaving her face alone concealed. The boy trembled violently, his tongue seemed to grow double its size and he felt a strange sickening sensation.

Perfectly passive in his master's hands, the page suffered his trousers to be taken down till they hung at his heels and himself to be projected on the bed. The libidinous baronet then took the lad's prick which was swollen and stiff in his hand and said:

'Get upon her, William, I shall put your cock into her for you and she shall take your maidenhead, if you have never fucked a woman.'

Miss Birchem did not speak in order that her voice should not betray her, but as she felt the youth getting between her quivering thighs, she raised her cunt towards him and in another instant her lover had plunged within her that which seemed like a bar of red hot iron, as his virile member was so fearfully stiff and burning.

Carried away by his own keen feelings, William commenced to lunge spasmodically at her and he was no sooner in to the root than he was rendered incapable, owing to the intensity of his pleasure, of resisting anything that might be done to him.

His master separated his legs and placed them on each side of his mistress' thighs, who immediately closed hers and thus kept the boy's prick firmly imbedded there. Arranging their relative positions, they both soon ran a course of the most luxurious and salacious enjoyment imaginable.

Leaning over the bed, Sir Clifford watched with looks of wild lust the to and fro motion of his prick within the moist folds of his mistress' cunt.

The moisture slowly oozed out at each thrust and, maddened by the sight, the baronet commenced to suck the testicles of his page, ever and anon allowing his tongue to glide by the side of this prick within the moist and slipping orifice of the cunt he was fucking.

Very shortly his master found by the swelling of the muscles and the increased stiffness of the prick that the youth was about ready to spend, which caused him to redouble his exertion and, when the crisis overtook them, their mutual spending oozed out and flowed into his delighted mouth.

After a momentary pause, to his great delight the page recommenced fucking the lovely palpitating body below him.

For some considerable time the intercourse between the trio was kept up, till Sir Clifford again desired a change, and as Miss Birchem wished to extend her field of amorous operations, a school was taken for her, which she was carrying on, at the time she is here introduced.

CHAPTER III
Mr Spanker

Miss Birchem whipped the bottom of Miss Wynne till Harry Staunton spent into her and his prick grew too limp to give her pleasure any longer, and when the governess released the flagellated girl from the position in which she had held her, she herself rose from Harry's lap.

Unsatisfied with the amount of pleasure he had given her – had they been alone he would have had his prick violently frigged by her – but seeing Julia's looks of unsatisfied desire raised by the tingling on her bottom she promised that the maid should have some pleasure.

The governess then took the virgin on her lap, taking care that their naked flesh should be in contact, and gradually raising her shift in front, told Harry to kneel before the lovely girl.

Then this lewd woman placed the young gentleman's head on Julia's naked thighs, and

213

instructed him how to gamahuche her and this he did, holding the handsome damsel convulsively by the thighs, while his tongue went in and out, the point of it being directed at her clitoris.

Julia soon was in heavenly rapture, she held his head forward to her burning quim with all her strength, her body quivering with emotion, her eyes half blinded by the humidity that came over them.

While Harry was thus occupied in giving pleasure to Julia, Miss Birchem lowered his trousers and by the pliant use of her busy fingers soon produced an erection, and increased the ardour with which he ravenously sucked the young and moist cunt of Julia.

Shortly the lecherous nymph let her head fall back, her eyes closed and her whole form was convulsed, while her lovely liquor of love oozed forth into the delighted mouth of her gamahucher. As soon as she had recovered, the eager governess took the lad between her thighs and made him fuck her.

While this proceeding was going on, it so happened that Mr Spanker, a gallant horse-dealer, was strolling through the meadows, thinking of the beauties of young Julia's mamma, whose naked beauties he was accustomed to enjoy in the privacy of her own room.

Behind the hedge against the bank on which Miss Birchem had seated herself, while Julia was sucked by young Harry, Mr Spanker had witnessed Harry's frigging and subsequent fucking of the ruttish governess.

The scene had been too much for him, for while busy Harry was piercing the damsel's cunt with his tongue, he had spent incontinently. Therefore he feared to make his presence known, as he feared his prick would not second his desires.

Leaving them therefore the horse-dealer went home. But before he reached home, the remembrance of what he had seen caused his prick to stiffen, and immediately on his arrival he was compelled to seek his wife whom he found dressing.

The buxom proprietress of the house was speedily divested of stays and shift, and lay on the bed with her thighs around her husband's neck, who was frantically forcing his tongue up her bottom-hole.

Afterwards Mr Spanker took himself from his wife's embrace just as she was commencing to spend from the excitement this luxurious proceeding caused her and, burying his erect prick within her cunt, he fucked her furiously, and she so enjoyed the unexpected attack that she aided his efforts by every means in her power.

After he had spent, the rake left his

unsatisfied wife for the arms of Mrs Wynne, whose embraces he lusted for more than ever since he had seen her daughter's naked beauties and the amorous joy she had experienced. Mrs Spanker had therefore to be satisfied with a nephew who was staying in the house and whom she determined to lure by remaining in the same state her husband had left her.

After frigging herself, she rose with the intention of dressing and seeking Augustus and bringing him to her bedroom under pretences of romping with him, till her young nephew should find himself held between her legs.

Then this shameless matron would tickle the young man's prick and afterwards take it out. Wriggling till her clothes were above her belly, she would force his stiff cock within her and obtain by force the fucking she was dying for.

But at the moment Mrs Spanker heard Augustus pass her door. Hastily opening it, nearly naked as she was, her white breasts completely bare, her back and shoulders only covered by her long hair, her legs naked more than halfway up, she called him in.

In a few minutes, the ruttish woman was on her bed, her chemise removed, and her legs around her nephew of sixteen, his fine prick within her, and both their bodies vibrated with the throbs of heavenly agony.

Meanwhile her husband was at Mrs Wynne's house, but that lady not expecting him had gone out to keep an assignation with another lover, in whose company she was spending her time between the sheets of a downy bed. Her daughter Julia, however, had reached their house some time before.

When Mr Spanker arrived, he found her in the drawing room, scarcely recovered from the confusion of her senses caused by the novel and delicious occupation in which she had been engaged. As they were old friends, she was soon sitting on his knees.

Feeling something hard pressing against her the young puss, more knowing than before since the lesson the governess had taught her, laid her hand upon it, artlessly enquiring: 'Oh! What is that? Surely a mouse inside your pocket?'

'Put your hand in, and feel the mouse,' said the horse-dealer. She allowed him to insert her hand inside his trousers. When her naked fingers touched his burning prick, she gave it a squeeze, and then drew her hand out, saying: 'It is not a mouse, it has no hair on it.'

'You only felt its nose, darling, look here,' and he drew his rod out completely. She got off his lap, her eyes sparkling as if with curiosity to see the little thing. He stood up, unfastened all the buttons, and exhibited not only his stiff prick, but the balls covered with hair.

'Gracious! What can this be for?' said the little maid artlessly.

'I shall show you, darling,' said Mr Spanker and, sitting down again with his legs wide open, he drew her between them. He then with little difficulty succeeded in raising her clothes and, placing his finger in her cunt, commenced to frig her deliciously.

Julia kissed him passionately and, seizing his prick, pushed the skin up and down until he was on the verge of spending, then her lover seized her hand and dragged it away, at the same moment applying his prick to her quim, which was moist with excitement.

The lovely girl let her head fall on his shoulder, hiding her burning face. 'Oh, you darling, I must fuck you,' he muttered, then repeated the expression with increased emphasis, getting his prick a little farther within her, at each upward heave.

It gave her such delicious sensations that she assisted him by firmly bearing down her cunt upon his prick, though now and then she could not help ejaculating: 'Oh! It hurts me!' as he endeavoured to make his way upwards within her.

This happened every time Mr Spanker tried to get his arrow in beyond the nut. The lustful horse-dealer was indeed mad to take her maidenhead but feared he could not do it in this position.

There was no one in the house but the servant, and she was quite safe as he well knew. So he said to the luscious virgin: 'Let me take you upstairs, darling, and place you on a bed, it will then go quite into you and will not hurt.

'Take me then,' said Julia, 'for I want so much for you to do it to me.' He took her up to her mother's bedroom and, placing her on the edge of the bed, he again raised her clothes and could not resist for a moment sucking that lovely juicy cunt.

Then as the compliant nymph lay there, her whole body palpitating with desire, her lovely eyes fixed on the stiff prick about to perforate her, her adorer placed a pillow under her bottom, and raised her cunt on a level with his prick.

Spreading her thighs wide asunder and getting in between them, Mr Spanker drew so close to her that his prick touched her cunt. Separating the pink lips with his thumb and finger, he guided his burning rod into her narrow quim and then began the fucking that was doomed to destroy her virginity.

'Put your legs over my back, darling,' demanded the lascivious horse-dealer.

Julia did so and with his assistance her pretty thighs formed a resting place for his head, her knees were at his neck, and her legs hung over his back. This position stretched her cunt open to its utmost extent and every thrust he now gave drove him deeper within her.

The violated maid murmured: 'Oh! Your cock! It is too large, and so stiff it hurts, but so deliciously.'

'Bite my neck, darling girl,' cried her seducer, 'I am going into you, and one more thrust will do it.'

The lascivious damsel did so, and then was pierced to the quick and her cunt inundated with the hot spunk which rushed from the great prick within her.

Her virginity was now destroyed. She closed her eyes, and lay still when her lover withdrew, her buttocks alone giving an occasional spasmodic heave as the white spunk issued forth in precious drops.

Julia then arose and threw herself upon Mr—Spanker's arm, hiding her face in his bosom, while her seducer lovingly caressed her now womanly cunt.

CHAPTER IV
Julia

Keenly desirous after this to enjoy the amorous girl at full leisure and in a state of nudity, Mr Spanker made her promise to meet him on the following day at his apartments, when he would take her to a house of assignation and fuck her naked.

Her seducer would not attempt then nor afterwards to fuck Julia under the room of her mamma for, fond as that lady was of voluptuous pleasure, she might not approve of her daughter being fucked.

He also wished to give her lovely posteriors such a flagellation as he had seen Miss Birchem bestow on her beautiful bum. Julia actually kept her appointment, and assumed an attire more appropriate to her as she was no longer a virgin.

Her stepfather, for her mamma had married twice, had noticed how the gentlemen fixed their eyes on Julia's legs, and how they evidently lusted for her, on seeing the rounded outlines of her well developed legs.

He had therefore insisted that she should wear longer skirts. New dresses having been made for her, she had put one of them on this day for the first time, but not before the exhibition of her lovely limbs had caused her to have received another fucking.

Towards the evening of the previous day, and after Mr Spanker had taken her maidenhead, the fickle girl thought she would like to see if Harry Staunton was looking for her in the lane where their previous encounter had taken place.

She therefore wandered thither, and was very near the same spot, close to a gate that led into a field covered with wild flowers. Here Sir Clifford chanced to see her. He accosted her, for the moment being very desirous to possess so beautiful a girl.

The enamoured baronet asked where the path through the fields led to, and on her informing him, he so overwhelmed her with compliments on her loveliness that her face was suffused with blushes and she seemed panting with excitement.

The nobleman then asked her to go with him so that he might not lose himself. Julia readily consented. It was necessary to climb over a gate and the gallant baronet assisted the alluring maid to mount it. As she stepped up, his eyes were gloating on her fine limbs.

When he helped her to throw her leg over the top bar, he not only contrived that her dress should be so disarranged that a portion of her thigh should be uncovered, but that his hand should slip upwards on her warm flesh till it reached her quim.

When he touched the warm lips of her quim, her sensations were indescribably exquisite. 'Let me get over on the other side to help you, my dear,' said this chivalrous man, and Julia blushed assent.

Giving an emphatic pressure to her velvet cunt, the eager baronet leaned over, holding his arms out to receive her. She jumped, her clothes flying up and disclosing her young charms as he caught her. The grass was tall and well covered with daisies and golden buttercups.

Thinking he would follow her, the tantalising girl ran some distance and commenced to cull the flowers, her face flushing and her bosom rising with sensual emotion. Her admirer was very soon by her side and, pretending to pluck wild flowers also, selecting those apparently that were by her dress.

But as her legs were wide open as she stooped his hand had little or no difficulty in finding her tempting little cunt, into which he quickly inserted his finger. As he touched her excitedly on the clitoris, she fell forward on his arm while he continued to frig her.

The voluptuous girl let her fair young face rest on his shoulder and she acutely enjoyed the pleasure he was causing her. Without any diminution of the activity with which he manipulated her moist cunt, Sir Clifford then took out his prick and asked her to fondle it.

'So,' enquired Julia, as she chafed his magnificent cock with her dainty fingers, till he was on the point of coming, while her own eyes betrayed that she was fast approaching a similar condition. He would have preferred to check his own and her emission, so that he might have enjoyed her to the full and ravished her thoroughly.

It was however impossible, and the libidinous baronet was compelled to send his spending over Julia's hand while she, under the friction of his finger, gave way to her sensations, spending exquisitely and sighing deeply as she spent.

When they had recovered Sir Clifford still wished to fuck her, and therefore begged her to come to the farther corner of the field where they would be altogether unobserved. She readily consented. He helped her to rise, for she had sunk on the grass for him to frig her, and they went away together.

When he had laid the appetising maid down on a bank which formed a natural couch, the libertine unfastened the front of her dress and, liberating her breasts, began to tickle and squeeze the nipples.

Seeing how excited she became, the voluptuary gradually raised her dress and fastening his lips to the lips of her cunt, all wet and moist as it was from her recent spending. This debaucher sucked her luscious quim amorously and licked her clitoris, which was now fully erect and hard, till Julia again profusely emitted into his mouth.

This caused his prick to become stiff and burning. Placing himself between her thighs, the baronet put the scarlet head of his rod in the rosy opening of her body and, placing both his hands beneath and parting the cheeks of her bottom, he raised her slightly towards him.

The fornicator sent his prick in up to the hilt and commenced to thrust it backwards and forwards. Suddenly they heard the sound of footsteps but as they evidently proceeded from the other side of the hedge they knew they could not be seen, so continued their lovely occupation.

Sir Clifford and his luxurious companion heard however that the newcomers evidently were reclining behind the hedge, and also they were members of the opposite sex. Suddenly Julia whispered: 'It is my mother and her nephew.'

Mrs Wynne and her young nephew evidently were also bent on pleasure for, after the sound of kissing had been heard, a lascivious sound succeeded, from which it was very evident they were either gamahuching or fucking.

'It is coming,' murmured Mamma. 'So is mine,' uttered the nephew. This had such an effect on the daughter that she became frantic, and spent in almost agonised convulsions, bathing the prick of the baronet with the pearly dew.

Sir Clifford and Julia now separated, but the young lady was more madly lewd than before and hastened to the house of Mr Spanker. When she arrived there she threw herself in his arms and he, placing her in an easy chair, knelt in front of her and gave her a hasty taste of bliss.

After which they started for the house of assignation in order that the bottom of the debauched girl might be birched and she initiated into all the wild excesses of lust, and all kinds of whipping lubricity.

Julia was by now fully conscious of her prurience. A large number of men and women delight to practise flagellation in all its forms as an accompaniment or as an inducement to love's paroxysm, cruelty creating an intense sensual excitement in some when holding under physical domination a creature of the opposite sex.

There was no doubt for the lecherous maid that her seducer also possessed this mania, and the pain he was about to inflict upon her would lend additional zest to their mutual enjoyment in that house of assignation which they were bound for.

It was in fact a brothel where rods and whips are kept in reserve to use on the posteriors of the customers or the delicate charms of the venal nymphs, according to wishes expressed and paid for, while the voluptuary gives large sums to the procuress to ravish tremulous virgins.

CHAPTER V
The House of Flagellation

As she entered the room in which the operations were to take place, Julia was influenced by various emotions, but her temperament was such that the lascivious sensations she had experienced already inflamed her lust to a greater extent than would otherwise have been the case.

The chamber of flagellation contained a large bedstead with a bed of down. From the posts and other points were heavy, silk cords that were used for tying the person to be birched in an extended position so that the effect might be seen by the operator in the most perfect manner.

There were also velvet pillows that might be placed between the thighs, so that the friction and soft contact of the velvet might assist the victim to spend while undergoing flagellation. An ardent curiosity and the desire of amorous pleasures drove the wanton damsel almost mad with suppressed expectation.

Around the room were whipping machines of varied construction. One was made in such a manner that when tied up, the back was in a horizontal position, whilst there projected from the lower part a dildo long enough to reach and penetrate the quim.

Another whipping machine was like a rocking-horse, on which the woman was stretched on her face, her legs embracing the sides of the machine. Every chair was of a different pattern, and had its own special use, being devoted to some special form of lust, and intended for the gratification of a special whim.

Mr Spanker explained the use of these various things, and his young mistress grew every moment more madly lewd, until at last she was ready to undergo anything. Her seducer now commenced to remove her hat and jacket, and then to unbutton the bosom of her dress, releasing her panting bubbies.

With these he toyed for a while, until she herself proceeded to rid herself of every article of clothing, and was very shortly standing before him in a state of perfect nudity. The horse-dealer followed her example and, seizing her by the lower part of her body, his bare arm between her thighs, he lifted her on the bed.

The debauchee then extended the panting girl on her belly, fastening her hands in velvet bands which were attached to the silken cords hanging from the upper end of the bed and firmly securing them to the two posts. He then extended her legs in a like manner, fastening her feet to the lower posts by similar appliances.

Heavens what a sight was thus presented to him! Her white and palpitating flesh throbbed, and every muscle was strained to the utmost. Her lovely breasts could be seen under her elevated arms, and the distension of her legs enabled the interior of her moist cunt to be perfectly seen, her clitoris quite stiff and red.

The lovely anus too could be seen, nestling between the rounded cheeks of Julia's bottom. Having manipulated it for some time, this salacious man eagerly stooped down, and licked the full white bottom all over. Thrusting his nose into the furrow, he then placed his tongue for a moment in the nether orifice, after postillioning it with two fingers.

After the voluptuary had tongued the utmost recesses of her fundament and wetted it amply with his saliva, which made her moan with pleasure, he then placed his hands under the beautiful creature. He felt her juicy cunt with one hand and gently frigged her, while he rubbed her nipples with

231

the other hand till she was on the verge of spending. Then he ceased and watched with gloating eyes the spasm that convulsed every fibre of her coral slit.

The tormentor now selected a pliant birch, and commenced to flog her gently on the buttocks and inside of the thighs, gradually increasing the force of the blows till all began to tingle and grow red.

Miss Wynne bounded at each blow, screaming it was too much and too hard. Mr Spanker then ceased for a moment and, inserting one finger in her hot vulva, gently frigged her again, while he birched with the other arm in such a manner as to excite rather than hurt.

Julia was overwhelmed by an unknown delicious sensation. This caused her to undulate her back and raise her buttocks as well as circumstances would permit to meet the falling lash. Her tormentor now grew frantic, and increased the force of his blows to such an extent as to make her cry out: 'Oh you do hurt me, it is cutting into my flesh!'

This brought into the room the buxom proprietress of the house of flagellation. He motioned to her not to discover herself, and she accordingly watched with glaring eye and inflated nostril the exciting scene that was being enacted, till she was obliged to raise her clothes and commence to frig her quim.

The procuress was half mad with voluptuousness. Her knees trembled and her uncovered breasts heaved violently. Wriggling her body in all directions she widened her thighs and heaved her bottom till, throwing herself on the whipping machine with the dildo, she caused it to enter her vagina, and by the energy of her motions soon covered it with her spendings.

In the meantime Julia cried out: 'Oh! Flog me harder! Do anything! I am mad with my feelings.'

She felt no more pain, only the most intoxicating pleasure, and soon died away in all the agony of a final rapture: 'Oh heavens! My bottom, my cunt, it is coming, I am going to spend!'

With a howl of pleasure, the lewd girl discharged copiously, her lovely pink bumhole opening and closing with each thrust of the loins, in which the cheeks of her bottom hardened with the contraction consequent on the spasm passing through her.

While his luxurious mistress lay half insensible, Mr Spanker unscrewed the dildo from the whipping machine and, reeking as it was with the spunk that had just been shed on it, gently pressed it into Julia's arsehole and fast moved the artificial member backwards and forwards.

Her whole body stiffened and the lovely girl seemed like one convulsed, so marvellous was the effect on her erotic nature. While her lover was withdrawing again the magnificent *godemiché*, and placing it up her sweet cunt, she commenced the up and down movement of her body to frig herself with it involuntarily.

The lady of the house of flagellation now begged Mr Spanker to birch her. She had stripped and was lying on a couch constructed in such a manner that the velvet fitted every curve of her body, belly downwards. He advanced to the upper end of the couch and, leaning a little forward, commenced to flagellate her violently.

This soon excited her again, and she seized his bursting penis and, nestling it between her lips, sucked it luxuriously, contracting the muscles of her mouth around the palpitating member, at the present moment raised to its full length, and pushed her head to and fro till he spent with the wildest contortions and a copious discharge sent her into an agony of delight.

The lewd procuress then looked up at her tormentor pleadingly, the lovely drops of sperm still hanging about her lips, and he bent down and kissed her fervently, receiving back into his own mouth some of the dew he had spent in hers.

Mr Spanker then fondled her firm thighs and curly-haired mound, and rubbed violently the glaring red point all smooth and moist. Frigging her luscious fanny with the palm of his hand, he speedily brought on the crisis. With a spasmodic contraction of her buttocks, she shot out a flood of thick, pearl-coloured spunk over his hand, and lay for several minutes soaking with bliss.

When this was concluded, they perceived that Julia was watching them intently. 'Oh! said she, 'do come to me again, do not leave me.'

'You shall have a new pleasure, darling,' said her lover, 'and our friend here shall initiate you.'

Rising from the couch, the Madame came and lay on the bed beside the girl in a reversed position, and commenced to kiss her bottom and tickle her clitoris.

Then, passing one leg over her prostrate body, her cunt pressed hard against Julia's loins, she buried her head between her thighs and gamahuched her luxuriously, pushing a finger gently up her anus and causing her the most divine pleasure.

After this, Julia was released, and they all sat side by side and partook of champagne and other refreshments. Mr Spanker then said that he must be birched in order to make his shaft stand again, and the fair Julia had the satisfaction of flagellating his bottom till his enormous prick stood like iron.

Then, rising hastily he placed the proprietress in an easy chair, which being unfolded made her fall backwards so as to lie horizontally with his knees, the chair being high enough to bring her quim on a level with his rampant pego now exhibited at full stretch. Her legs were then elevated, with her feet tossing about in the air.

In this position the buxom lady of the house was fucked, till they both spent in the wildest ecstasy, Julia all the time flogging his backside, while a torrent of boiling sperm was shed into the bawd's womb. A lovely waiting maid, who had entered during this occurrence, was now seized, thrown on her belly on a chair and her clothes tossed up.

She was fucked up her bottom-hole by Mr Spanker, while Julia sucked madly at the relaxed quim of the salacious procuress and then, embracing the spending woman, forcibly rubbed her excited button and cunt up against hers. She brought on such a spasm of delight that not only their grottos, mounds and bellies, but also their thighs, arses and buttocks were wetted with their united abundant spendings, till they fell on the floor utterly exhausted.

Shortly after, the horse-dealer and his young mistress left the house of flagellation. But an appointment was made for the following Monday . . .

CHAPTER VI
Annie

A very pretty girl of graceful figure walking through Jermyn Street, was accosted by a gentlemanly young man who, after some conversation of a character highly flattering to herself and which completely won the confidence of her guileless heart, persuaded her to accompany him to his chambers, which were close by.

When they arrived he brought out wine and biscuits which he persuaded her to take. Sitting on a luxurious sofa under the influence of the wine and his fascination, she became so enamoured of him that when he put his arm around her waist and, drawing her closely to him, pressed warm kisses on her pouting lips she was so overcome as to return them; nor was she able to resist when he began to take further liberties with her.

The young man pressed her to him, and with a little difficulty got his hand inside the bosom of her dress and pressed the warm and firm globes that nestled there. The pretty girl struggled slightly and said: 'Oh! You must not! Don't, do let me alone.'

'I don't wish to let you alone,' said the young gallant. 'You must let me feel this soft and enchanting bosom, you must indeed.'

Saying this, he managed to unfasten her dress completely, and actually got out one naked globe in his hand which he devoured with kisses and so disordered all her senses that, while her breasts were fluttering under the wanton encroachments of his hand which was now moulding her bubbing bubbies into all sorts of forms, he succeeded also in gradually raising her dress sufficiently high to enable him to place the other hand between her thighs, up which he gradually groped till he reached the silken covering of the spot where they joined.

This alarmed her at first and she tried hard to remove his hand but, getting his fingers between the velvet lips of her warm slit, he began to frig her and this lustful action rendered her powerless. The panting girl yielded herself entirely, and lay back in his arms, her head upon his shoulder, her eyes half closed, her lips moving in unison with his as he kissed her.

The young Don Juan saw she was in no condition to resist him, even if he fucked her.

He therefore drew forth his prick, hot and swollen as it was, and throwing one leg over her, he brought his stiff cock close enough to her to enable him to bring the bursting head among the floss that covered the entrance to her juicy cunt.

Now, while maintaining the progress he had made, he shifted her into a better position for enjoying her. Shifting her head to the pillow on the couch, he laid one of her legs on that substitute for a bed and, getting between them, he brought the other up also, and then lay down on the body of the panting girl, whose face was now flushed with the deep crimson of desire.

He all the time was stopping her entreaties by his constant kisses on her half open mouth, while his arms were pressing around her loins. Already the dreadful shaft was pressing its way to its utmost length into the luscious gap of her quim, while she was opening and extending her legs of her own accord so as to enable him to penetrate her better.

Suddenly, the tremulous maid was horrified to see the door open, and another gentleman enter the room. With a look of such genuine shame that she could not have imagined it mere acting, her lover disengaged himself from her endearing arms and rose from her form, which thus became exposed to the sight of the intruder, leaving her to cover as best she could her private parts.

This she could not readily accomplish, as her lover had contrived to entangle his foot amongst her drapery. The intruder was thus enabled to gain her side before she could recover an upright position and cover herself up. This he prevented her doing, holding her clothes as she attempted to pull them down, and at the same time pressing her backwards in the position in which she lay before.

The trembling girl was alarmed, as the intruder's stern voice was heard saying: 'So Sir, this is the way you bring young ladies here in my absence. Leave the room, Sir. As for you, Miss, I shall keep you here as you are, and send for your friends whom I know, in order that they may see how you behave, when away from them.'

The errant lover slunk away and left the room, and the frightened girl felt as though she could have sunk through the floor, as the intruder still kept her clothes up when they were left alone. She entreated him to let her go but he would not, and after gloating for a while on her charms, he said: 'I shall either expose you or give you a good birching for your wickedness. Choose which it shall be.'

After a few moments she, in her confusion and fright, chose the latter alternative. He then allowed her to rise and, taking a birch from a cupboard that stood in the room, the tormentor sat down. Stretching out his legs before him, he bent her across them, her fair head hanging down as if to hide her face, while submitting to such a punishment as she was about to receive.

The cruel gentleman then gratified himself by birching her posteriors, enjoying her sighs, which she gave vent to, as the process of the whipping gradually brought back that lustful heat in her quim which the blandishments of her betrayer had first generated there, and these sighs soon became more expressive of voluptuous passion than of any other feeling.

Before he had birched her up to that point when the man feels he must fuck the flagellated one, or let his spunk flow in his trousers, the panting maid was as willing as he was that her flagellator should enjoy her in front, as well as behind. Throwing the rod aside, he took her in his arms and begged that she would make friends with him, saying that he could not resist flogging her, when he saw another enjoying her lovely charms.

While she was in this excited state she could not resist his appeal to allow him to fuck her. When his hand was laid on her cunt, he elevated it with a significance that her arch smile made still more tempting. Kissing her ardently, he at once placed her on the couch in the same position in which he had found her, and placed himself between her extended thighs.

His enormous prick speedily entered her, and he commenced to move backwards and forwards, until with spasmodic action they both yielded up love's exquisite stream. He then got off, but would not allow her to rise, sitting by her side and toying with her beautiful limbs. After some little time, he pulled a bell within reach, and she heard approaching footsteps, begging him at the same time to allow her to cover her nakedness.

This he refused to allow, and when his page entered he showed him where his priapus had just entered, and their united spendings still oozing from it. 'I must make you amends for having deprived you of your sweetheart, even if it was only for a time. I have been enjoying her, but I cannot even now spare her from my sight,' said he, 'so if you fuck her, it must be while I watch you. I am sure she will allow me that pleasure.'

By this time the girl was too wanton to object and, in order to carry out their scheme more thoroughly, they took her to a place more calculated for practising lechery. The gentleman was Sir Clifford Norton and the page the same William who had shared with him the lascivious body of Miss Birchem, and it was by Sir Clifford's order that William had gone out in search of a pretty girl.

Miss Annie found herself in the bedroom of the baronet. The first thing they did was to undress her to her corset and the next to strip off all their own clothing. Annie was asked to sit at the foot of the bed, then they tucked up her chemise and fastened it up in order that her lovely cunt and thighs might be fully exhibited.

William laid on his back on the bed and his stiff cock was grasped by Sir Clifford who was manipulating it in order that Annie might receive it in her body while in a state of glorious excitement. They had taken up the birch, as the lustful maid was by now fully conscious that flagellation creates an intense sensual thrill and is the best inducement to love's paroxysm, as she had experienced by herself when flogged by the baronet.

Now Annie was castigating the baronet's posteriors with the birch as he leant over the bed, frigging his page. After this had continued for some time, the lewd girl threw herself on her back on the bed, and they both gloated over her glowing charms, their stiff pricks throbbing and rising at each pulsation of the blood swelling through their veins.

William then grasped her bubbies, squeezing the erect nipples until she moaned with delight. Sir Clifford fiercely rubbed her clitoris which was now crimson and hard. The page then mounted above the panting and moaning girl, and as she pressed him tightly in her arms the baronet guided William's throbbing prick into her gaping vulva. When the pego was fairly in, the ruttish wench closed her thighs over him, and for a while gave herself wholly up to her lascivious feelings.

Annie was exciting her imagination by looking at Sir Clifford's priapus, whose immense shaft was dreadfully erect, with the glowing red head uncovered and all the flesh of the froenum well stretched. The baronet in turn watched the page's rammer with the keenest interest as it now disappeared within fair Annie's labouring body, and now reappeared in all its glory, as William withdrew it from its narrow cavity only to send it again, with still greater vigour and delight, into the utmost recesses of her streaming vagina.

The whim then seized the luxurious maid that she should like to have them both at once upon her, and like a queen of love whose word was law she bade Sir Clifford to mount behind the page that they might both have her at once. The baronet instantly obeyed her, but whether his penis would not reach so far as her cunt or whether he found a greater attraction elsewhere, it is certain that his giant tool found a resting place before it reached her greedy cunt.

Annie could see quite well what was taking place between the nobleman and his page. William's eyes were nearly starting from his head with a flush of heated lust upon each feature, while Sir Clifford looked as though his lascivious gratification was literally burning him up. The scene continued till the voluptuous girl felt a flood of hot sperm bursting into her, and found her own passions so affected by it that she also gave way to her feelings, which utterly overcame her.

They then arose and sat down by the fire. After some lascivious toying, they took off the chemise and corsets which Annie had retained until now, and the libidinous baronet, whose prick was again intensely stiff, took her upon his lap, impaling her upon his upright shaft. While he fucked her, the pretty girl frigged the cock of the page and amorously played with his balls, tickling the rosy foreskin and squeezing the hard testicles nestling in his corrugated scrotum.

William was excited to the utmost, and how eloquent of pleasant emotion were the eyes of Annie as she received the full discharge of the baronet's spunk into her glorious cunt, while the creamy jet from the page spouted forth over her caressing fingers.

Once more they prepared to roger the girl, this time on the bed again.

William lay on his back, Annie above him, while Sir Clifford stood by the side of the bed, frigging himself and watching them in the ecstasy of coition. Then in his excitement the page seized the baronet's penis and frigged him, while still fucking Annie, with a vigour that seemed to increase as her delightful quim grew hotter and randier.

With a bewitching voice, the lecherous maid gave expression to her wantonness, repeating after them the most bawdy terms conceivable. All this so maddened Sir Clifford that his body was pervaded with fuck. He then brought out a rod and lashed the heaving buttocks of the lascivious girl, who in the abundance of her pleasure, challenged him to flog and fuck her till she fainted dead away.

As she goaded them into a fury that could only be quenched by their smothering her with spunk, the page soon made his spendings fly into her belly and directed the full stream of the baronet's profuse discharge over her flagellated backside. Still their desires for the voluptuous girl were not quenched, although their weapons were for the time incapable of standing.

Annie exerted all her fascination to arouse them, kissing their bodies and private parts, sucking their luscious knobs, toying with their foreskins and hairy balls, and giving up every portion of her body to them, making them kiss and suck her breasts, titillate her rosy nipples, lick her still nervously throbbing cunt and corrugated brown arsehole.

Lying on her back, Annie showed them all the graceful curves her undulating form and beauteous limbs could offer, while they enacted with her all the voluptuous dalliance that so exquisite a figure could incite them to. Presently she leapt up and cried: 'If you cannot fuck my fanny again, if a naked woman will not excite you sufficiently, show me what you can do together.'

'Come, Sir,' said the salacious maid, addressing the baronet, 'place yourself like a woman, and see what your page can do for you, and if he cannot do more for you than for me, I will flog him till he cannot stand.'

Sir Clifford now extended himself on his belly, opened his thighs and buttocks, and made William mount up behind.

Annie now guided the page's penis into his master's anus, holding the lower part of it, while she administered such a birching to both cheeks of his bottom, as soon caused the shaft to stand as stiff as ever. She watched the pego now gradually make its way within the narrow aperture between the cheeks of the baronet's bottom until it was buried to the root.

They then went through that sport for which Sir Clifford had so keen a relish, affording to Annie the most intense delight. As the nobleman tossed and writhed on the bed, the wicked girl secured his enormous prick and, squeezing it as hard as she forcibly could, she chafed the glowing instrument from root to point, with almost demonic energy.

The baronet spent with a scream of mingled pain and pleasure, and at the same moment received the spunk of his page in the innermost recesses of his arse, while the girl, mad with voluptuousness, grasping the palpitating lips of her fanny and fiercely rubbing her throbbing clitoris, indulged in the most intoxicating lasciviousness.

After this bout, Sir Clifford dismissed Annie with a handsome present, and arranged a future meeting, which the delighted girl promised them both to attend.

A LADY OF QUALITY

*A romance
of lust*

ANONYMOUS

Even on the boat to France, Madeleine
experiences a taste of the pleasures that await
her in the city of Paris. Seduced first by Mona,
the luscious Italian opera singer, and then, more
conventionally, by the ship's gallant British
captain, Madeleine is more sure than ever of her
ambition to become a lady of pleasure.

Once in Paris, Madeleine revels in a feast of
forbidden delights, each course sweeter than
the last. Fires are kindled in her blood by the
attentions of worldly Frenchmen as, burning
with passion, she embarks on a journey of
erotic discovery . . .

FICTION/EROTICA   0 7472 3184 2   £2.99

CREMORNE GARDENS

ANONYMOUS

An erotic romp from the libidinous age of the Victorians

UPSTAIRS, DOWNSTAIRS . . . IN MY LADY'S CHAMBER

Cast into confusion by the wholesale defection of their domestic staff, the nubile daughters of Sir Paul Arkley are forced to throw themselves on the mercy of the handsome young gardener Bob Goggin. And Bob, in turn, is only too happy to throw himself on the luscious and oh-so-grateful form of the delicious Penny.

Meanwhile, in the Mayfair mansion of Count Gewirtz of Galicia, the former Arkley employees prepare a feast intended to further the Count's erotic education of the voluptuous singer Važelina Volpe – and destined to degenerate into the kind of wild and secret orgy for which the denizens of Cremorne Gardens are justly famous . . .

Here are forbidden extracts drawn from the notorious chronicles of the Cremorne – a society of hedonists and debauchees, united in their common aim to glorify the pleasures of the flesh!

FICTION/EROTICA   0 7472 3433 7   £3.50